Trust and Truths

GEM LARMAR

WRITTEN GEMS PUBLISHING

Ebook ISBN: 9781647044862

Back Cover Image: Margoe Edwards

Editor: Smokey Day

Front Cover Image and Design: Winnie Bean

www.writtengem.com

Contents

Acknowledgments

Prologue

I want so much to tell this guy why I'm so damaged, but fear he will no longer be interested in me. We're flirting back and forth in this messenger app, and I want to keep it going. Am I wrong for not being upfront?

"Yvonne, I feel there is something you want to tell me," Thomas types.

"There is, Thomas," I type as I fight to hold back tears. "I am living with HIV. I am HIV positive!"

There is a long pause, and I can't take it anymore. I slam my laptop shut, leaving Thomas with his thoughts about what I had just revealed about me. I get up from the desk, sobbing at this point and get into bed, laying in a fetal position, as I cry until finally, I'm asleep.

GEM LARMAR

I want to dedicate this book to two people who are no longer with us.

To my Grammy. I miss you lots and I wish you were here. You always said that your grandchildren will do great things no matter if it were big or small. This is for you.

Dad, we didn't see eye to eye, but you were there from our births till you passed. Sadly, a lot of kids didn't have a father in their lives, but you were there.

I hope where ever you both are, you're okay and are no longer suffering.

1

Don't Tell

Being a loner is something I've never dreamed of being at this stage of my life. I have friends and a mom who loves me very much, but even with the people who I adore around me, I still feel very alone.

I'm a very private person and have been holding on to something that I have not shared with anyone. Not even my best friends... Well, I didn't tell two of them, and that is I'm HIV positive, but undetectable.

I have been positive for years now and it has been hard when trying to date because, well, nobody wants this shit and who could blame them? I did tell Ming Song, who is the closest to me than the other two. We both share the same fate for our health, except she just found out she was positive only a few years ago. Many people think she is mean, and they are right. She can be. Ming has the "resting bitch face" down, but being positive, I guess, would make you resentful. She is overprotective of her friends, and she does not play any games. She says what's on her mind and doesn't really care how it comes out.

She's sitting on my bedroom floor with my other two friends, Cashmere and Karma, looking for the new movie that was just added to online streaming to watch.

Cashmere Paxton is the one that jokes around a lot. She can be funny in almost any situation, even a serious one. I'm not kidding. She would be the one to laugh at while at a funeral. Funny, always at the wrong time, I swear, but I love her anyway. I didn't, however, tell her about what I am going through, but she helps me when I am in a depressive state. She is outgoing, the life of the party, and a huge flirt. I have never seen her cry so if something is going on with her; I do not know what it is, or she may just be good at hiding it and, like Ming, she has no filter.

The quietest in the group would be Karma Duncan. She is shy and most think she is a pushover. One of us is always there to rescue her when there is any kind of altercation. She is a sweetheart and the only one out of the four of us who's married. She loves talking about the zodiac and comparing our signs with our decisions, and when any of us are meeting someone new. I don't believe in it, but she does, and it's entertaining sometimes.

Then there is little ole positive me. I'm Yvonne Dent and like my friends, I am 37. Most people peg me to be immature and silly, but I can be serious too. Hell, these past few weeks I have been nothing but serious. When I am being playful, I use it to hide my true feelings and it's what keeps me from being down on most days; I think. I haven't been in a playful mood lately and I think my friends are starting to notice.

We all are sitting around snacking while looking for the new movie and discussing things we see on social media when I hear a loud crash. I run downstairs to see my mom has knocked over her cane. I didn't know a cane could make so much noise.

"Mom are you okay," I ask as I pick the cane up off the floor. You have to be more careful!

"Yvonne, stop treating me like I am some old woman," my mom retorts. "I'm only 57 and the reason I have a cane is that I was hurt thanks to the neighbor's enormous dog. I'm still thinking of suing her ass. That dog should have been on a leash!"

"Alright, alright, Mama, calm down. You know I want nothing to happen to you, sheesh."

"Yvonne, get up here! We found the movie to watch," yells Cashmere. "We want to start it now. Is everything okay down there?"

"Do you need anything else, Mama," I ask as I help her under the covers, ignoring Cash.

"No, sweetie," she answers with a long-drawn-out operatic yawn. "You go on upstairs and watch your movie. I'm tired and I'm going to sleep."

I kiss my mom good night on her forehead, and I walk out, pulling her bedroom door shut.

"Okay, what are we watching," I ask as I walk into my bedroom.

"It's the new one that just came on 'Homeflix'," Ming answers. "The one called 'The Two Tales', with that guy, you have been crushing on since he came upon the acting scene," she adds while giggling.

I roll my eyes and laugh while blushing. Thomas Edgar, a tall, dark-skinned, incredibly handsome man, at least in my eyes, that I have been eyeing ever since he came to Chicago, where there was an outside interview done with him about the new movie. He is new, but not really as he has done small parts in other popular movies. He is still new to me and after that interview, I just, I don't know, just... fell in love at first sight, maybe? All I know is he was being interviewed in Grant Park downtown and I was snacking before I raised my head to look up at what was taking place on that stage, and our eyes met.

I sigh as I think back. That "eyes meeting" thing only happened for a quick sec. A quick sec as in him thinking, "Okay, I see you, but back to the interview" like it was nothing special. And my quick sec was more like "He sees me and runs off of the stage in slow motion, then we embrace looking like 'googly eyed lovers' never letting go" sec. Regardless of whether he was feeling me, I decide to follow him on social media.

I remember it like it was yesterday. Me, having on my 'sluttiest' best... Okay, I'm kidding, but I looked damn good. I was hoping to get close enough to him after the interview to at least smile, wave or get a photo with him, but no such luck. The only close up I'm getting of this man is sitting in front of my 40-inch screen at home watching him in his movie.

"This movie is pretty good, huh," Karma asks.

Cashmere, the main one rushing me to get upstairs to start the movie, is face deep in her phone.

"Sure, it's ok, but we have to figure out who to hook Ming and Vonne up with so that we can all go to the couple's fair this time," Cashmere says while raising her head and looking directly at Ming and me.

"Oh my God, Cash," Ming snaps. "We will date when we are ready. Drop the shit already!"

"Shhhh, my mom is sleeping," I say in an angry whisper. "Ming is right, Cash. When we are ready, we will. Chill!"

I look from the tv to Cash and add, "and don't even think of trying to hook us up with anyone again, either."

"Oh, who could forget that fiasco," Ming says while rolling her eyes.

"Ugh! Fine, stay single and miserable," Cashmere mutters.

She then looks at us as if we are from another planet. I guess she has nothing else to say because she turns back to the movie.

I'm losing interest in the movie at this point and get up off the floor, walk over to my bed and sit, then decide to check my social media direct messages. I glance at my friends on the floor watching the movie but paying more attention to Cashmere. Here is my best friend wanting us to take part in something that Ming and I aren't too comfortable with. I feel bad about not sharing my secret with her, but then think maybe it is best I don't.

Getting back to my phone, I notice that Thomas Edgar had followed me back on social media, 'MediaPal'. I slowly lay back on my bed, not taking my eyes off the bright phone screen. When I see his profile, I stare at the message icon. Dare I do it? Finally, I think "what can go wrong"?

I send: *"Hi, I'm Yvonne. I saw your live interview downtown and love your work. Thank you for the follow back,"* with a 'smile' emoji.

As I'm putting my phone down, I hear a ping. I pick up the phone thinking it was going to be gratitude for the compliments I gave and all I get is an 'Okay' emoji. Oh well, he didn't have to respond at all, but he did.

I put my phone under my pillow, tell the ladies good night, and close my eyes while listening to the movie until I'm in dreamland.

***

Waking up first thing in the morning, I have to take these cute little colorful pills to keep me alive and healthy. A reminder about my health that I hate, but should be happy I am alive, right?

Since I am not working, the only way for me to survive is by collecting disability benefits. My mental state makes it hard for me to get a job and keep it. Even if it's not for the virus, they granted me disability for what the virus has done to me, like, for example, my major depression, suicidal thoughts and the constant hiding myself away from the world.

Looking at me, you wouldn't know that I'm sick at all. I'm pretty, tall, curvy, and look healthy. My aunt is constantly saying I could be a model, but I'm too shy for that and I try to keep my life private. I think if I were to tell someone that I'm positive, they will think I'm lying. When I was first diagnosed, I thought it was a death sentence. People say if a person was incredibly skinny, they had Aids and are dying. HIV and Aids are the same to most people, even to me. I have not researched it much because I detest thinking about it.

It's so hot outside that I decide I won't wear a wig today, and I pull my long, thick curly tresses into a low ponytail before going into the bathroom to get myself ready for the day. My friends are still sleeping and the movie we were watching last night has replayed itself again after the ending.

I come out of the bathroom to finish getting ready in my room and see that Ming is awake.

"I need to head out," Ming says, jumping out of a pile of blankets that are on the floor where she slept. "This was nice. A sleepover like when we were kids."

"It was," I say while smiling. "I'm so glad that we could do it. I know I don't come out much anymore."

"Trust me, I know," Ming says as she is getting her bag together. "I think you will soon enough. It took me a while too, but I know people handle their situations differently. You will come around and if those two can't understand it, they will just have to."

The two she is talking about are Cashmere and Karma, who's snoring lightly still on the floor.

"Are you on your way to work," I ask Ming?

"Yeah, I have two appointments that I will do from home," she answers.

She picks her bag up and hurls it over her shoulder. Ming is a therapist, and it's funny to me she would choose this profession since she has stated she would never go to a therapist for anything because it wouldn't help her in any way. I feel the same.

"Well, have a good day and call me later," I say to her as we head downstairs.

I can hear my mom in the kitchen making a lot of noise, with dishes clinking and cabinets opening and closing. She appears outside the kitchen doorway as Ming steps off the last step.

"I'm making omelets. Are you leaving already," my mom asks Ming.

"Hi Ms. Dent! I'm going to have to pass, but I promise next time," Ming says while giving my mom a peck on the cheek. "I'm working this Saturday."

"Well, alright."

She seems a bit disappointed but understands Ming's leaving and walks back into the kitchen to continue with breakfast.

I walk Ming out and lock up, then join my mom in the kitchen.

"Where are Cash and Karma," my mom asks. "They are going to have breakfast, right?"

"You know those two don't turn down food," I say with a laugh.

"Good, because there is plenty."

She sounds pleased that someone would appreciate the time spent in the kitchen. I tell my mom that I'm going to get them for breakfast and run upstairs.

"Hot breakfast awaits," I tell Karma and Cashmere as they walk by me, going downstairs.

"Good, because I am starving and the best food is when I don't have to cook it," Cashmere says as she runs ahead of Karma.

I'm going to eat after I message Thomas about that emoji response he sent to me last night. I sit down on the edge of my bed and look at my phone. As I look at the message that I left him and his response, I'm wondering why I even want to message this guy in the first place. Yes, he is a man that I'm suddenly crushing on, but I can't date him even if I wanted to. I think it is just something to do. Would I have gone this far if he wasn't an up-and-coming star? Yes. Him being a star has nothing to do with it. I just can't seem to stop myself from wanting to message him. So, I send:

"Good morning! Do you interact with fans or is this just a platform you use to only show us your work?"

I put my phone in my pocket because I'm not expecting a response and head back downstairs with everyone else to have breakfast.

"Well, ladies, what do you have planned on this beautiful Saturday morning," my mom asks while collecting used dishes and placing them in a sink full of suds.

"I plan to drag your daughter out of this house," says Cashmere. "I'm thinking of going up north to the little coffee place where we used to hang out. Rita has been asking about you, Vonne."

"We can do that. We have no more coffee here, anyway. A nice, iced frappe dripping with extra caramel over whipped cream sounds delicious right now."

"Can we all go later," asks Karma. "I need to run a few errands."

"Okay," Cashmere says with a huff and throwing her arms in the air, "but we are going later this evening when Ming gets done with her clients."

"Don't worry, Cash, we will be there," Karma says.

"Well, you will be there," Cashmere starts, "but will Vonne?"

I roll my eyes but say nothing because chances are I may decide not to go. It's hard for me to go out on short notice. I have to mentally prepare for these things.

"She will be there," my mom says to my friends who are studying me because of my silence.

"I hope so," says Cashmere, "because I really want her to come out with us. It's always only me, Karma and Ming and its four of us."

"I will try," I finally say with a sip of my orange juice, "but I won't make any promises."

"I need to get going," says Karma rising from the table. "Thanks for breakfast, Ms. Dent."

"Yeah, me too," Cashmere says as she does the same, but gives my mom a hug who is near the sink with dishes waiting. "It was delicious!"

"Thanks, you two. Maybe Ming will join us next time."

"I'll walk ya'll out," I say, rising last.

The three of us make our way to the front door, where we say our goodbyes and the two leave. I rejoin my mom in the kitchen to help with the dishes.

"Vonne, I'm not sure why you are so afraid to leave the house," my mom starts, "but you weren't always this way."

I sigh softly. "It's just something I'm going through and will get past hopefully."

"Whatever is going on, you know you can tell me, right?"

I want to tell my mom what is happening. I'm just not sure how she will handle it. Even though I hate to see her worry like this, I'm just not ready to have that conversation yet.

"I know, Mama."

We finish the rest of the dishes in silence.

***

It's around 2 p.m. now and I see a message from Thomas. As I'm clicking it open, I get another, but it is from Cashmere. I swipe her message to the side and go for Thomas's, which says:

"Hi. I answer my fans when I can. Hope you're well."

Then I reply: *"Do you have anything else going on? My friends and I watched 'The Two Tales' last night, and it was pretty good."*

'The Two Tales' is a movie about a woman who is trying to get back at an ex-boyfriend with a false rape accusation, and the ex is trying to return the favor by accusing his ex-girlfriend of abuse and vandalism, also a fake accusation. If one of their stories is believed in court, the kids will go to that parent, while the other is charged. Thomas plays the young girl's father, who is trying to get her to do the right thing.

I only saw the first thirty minutes of the movie since Cashmere ruined it by talking about dates for Ming and me. But of course, I won't tell him that.

Thomas replies: *"Well, I have some projects that I am working on, but I can't really talk about them. I am a hustler. You won't see the end of me. I'm always working on something."*

I reply: *"I can't wait to see. I'm sure they will be just as good as 'The Two Tales'."*

He sends a 'heart' and two 'praying hands' emojis. Well, that is what the hands look like to me and that's it. Our conversation over. I am happy about the reply. Most celebrities don't chat with fans, especially through private inboxes.

I read Cashmere's text message. She wants me to be at the coffee place by 4 this evening, but I look at the clock and I can see I won't be there by that time using public transportation. I want to opt out of going, but I know they will just say I am hiding in the house again. Just wish they knew what I am going through. I try to fight depression on my own because I refuse to go into why I am feeling this way with friends and family. Sometimes I feel alone and think that if there is a God, he is punishing me for something, or that I'm that one creation he regrets.

I look in on my mom and see her legs propped up on the footstool while on the phone talking about one of our neighbors. After getting her attention, I mouth the words "I'm leaving" while pointing to the door. She nods and goes back to her phone call. I grab my waist bag, wrap it around my waist, making sure my phone and keys are there, before leaving.

***

I finally get to the coffee shop a few hours later. It is very busy inside. There is a couple at one table giggling while the woman playfully feeds her male friend a small piece of donut. At another table, there is a man on his laptop sipping on coffee while on his phone and has a small stack of papers nearby. Now, he is the definition of multi-tasking. Finally, I find my friends, not far from "multi-tasker", with Cashmere and Rita laughing loudly about something while Ming rolls her eyes and Karma looking confused.

"Hey ladies," I say, while playfully tapping Cashmere on her shoulder and making a funny face when she turns to face me.

Her mouth falls open when she sees me. Yes, I'm here. Now pick up your face, girl.

"Oh my God, you came," she shouts. "I just knew you were at home about to call with an excuse not to be here."

"It took a lot to psyche myself up to get out the door, but I am here," I say as I am looking up at the wall menu.

"Hey there, Miss Vonne," says Rita, "long time."

Rita and I hug each other after we exchange greets. I haven't seen Rita since high school and now she has taken over the family business, which is this coffee shop.

"Hey! It sure is," I say. "Can I get a Frappe with extra caramel?"

"Sure thing, Vonne. Would you like a pastry to go with that?"

"No thanks," I say, checking my phone. "All the caramel I am asking for is my pastry."

We both giggle.

When I look at my phone, I see there is an appointment reminder for me to get labs done. I'm scheduled for Monday afternoon. Cashmere starts speaking, so I put my phone away.

"So, let's talk about last night," Cashmere says.

She looks at me and Ming. Cash has been bugging us to get dates so we can go to the yearly Couple's Fair, but Ming is more than irritated. She likes to do things in her own time and Cash is making it worse.

Rita sits down my Frappe and walks away to a man motioning her over to his table.

"Something is definitely off with you two and it's been a while that I noticed it," Cashmere continues. "I didn't say anything before, but I think we should talk about it now."

"Nothing is going on with me," Ming says, "and if it were, I don't have to tell you anything."

"But we are supposed to be friends," Cashmere says while scooting her chair closer to the table, then leans in to get close to Ming, who is sitting on the other side. "I'm just saying that we are here for you. You don't have to keep it to yourself. That goes for you too, Yvonne."

"Whoa," I say as I'm about to take a sip of my Frappe, "Cash, I know you mean well, but there is nothing going on and you should just drop it."

"I can see that there, --."

Suddenly, Cashmere is interrupted by Ming scooting her chair back loudly and getting up from her seat with purse in hand.

"I'm out of here," she snaps.

As Ming turns to head for the exit, Karma and I rise, but Karma is closer, allowing her to quickly grab her arm.

"Wait! No, don't go," Karma pleads, as she tries to stop our friend, who looks as if she could kill Cashmere just by looking at her.

"It's really not that serious, Ming," Cashmere says while rolling her eyes. "The way you are acting right now, makes me think there is something going on."

"So just because something may be going on with me, I should tell you what the fuck it is?"

"Clearly you need to talk to someone. Look at how extra you are," Cashmere snaps.

"If I wanted you to know, Cash, your ass would know," Ming snaps back.

Poor Karma is standing at the table, still gripping on to Ming's arm, wide-eyed, at everything escalating so quickly. I don't know what my expression is, but I bet it's about the same as Karma's.

"Fine!" Ming looks directly at Cashmere and Karma. "You want to know what's going on!!! I am... I'm liv-- "

I'm thinking, is Ming going to tell them? Now... here at this coffee shop, in front of all these people. No, she can't! Not like this! I have to stop her. If she let that kind of information out, she will resent Cash for the rest of her life.

"That is enough," I yell while slamming my hand on the table. "This is not the time or the fucking place for this shit!"

All conversations, laughter, and dish noise stop and the coffee shop is so quiet you could hear a pin drop except for a few low coughs. But I'm pretty sure that the shop was quiet already when the explosion first started. I just didn't notice until now. All eyes are now on us.

Ming glares at Cashmere, then looks at me and Karma. She doesn't say another word and pulls her arm from Karma's grasp before storming out of the coffee shop.

"I'll talk to you all later," I say as I run after her.

I leave the coffee shop, but it's too late. Ming is already pulling out of her parking spot. I watch as she speeds down the street. With no way of stopping her, all I can do is stroll to the nearby bus stop so that I can catch the bus home.

2

Do We Need Cash?

I t is a stormy Monday morning and I'm trying to find something to wear for my doctor's appointment. I haven't spoken with the ladies since that horrible Saturday evening when we all were at the coffee shop and the big blowout happened.

There are a lot of messages on my phone. Mostly from Cashmere and Karma. I haven't heard from Ming, and I worry. I left a lot of text messages and a few voicemails, but I got nothing. Ugh! I am so pissed at Cashmere for that shit she started. I'm running late and I have a long bus ride to my appointment, so will just have to be pissed at her while I get ready.

I decide today, I'll wear a wig, so I put on my light brown wet and wavy. It will be perfect for today's rainy weather. I grab my light denim jacket, gray tank top, with light denim jeans and put them all on the bed. I head into the bathroom to shower. With so much on my mind, I stand under the hot water wondering how Ming is doing. We both are going through it and if I were in her shoes, I might've stopped talking to Cash for a long time, pulling a stunt like that in a crowded place. I break out of my deep thought and finish showering. I don't bother adding makeup since it's raining, and just put on a light brown shiny lip gloss and some mascara.

Now dressed and feeling good about my appearance, I go downstairs to find something light to eat before I leave. I'm more thirsty than hungry. I pour myself a glass of orange juice and take a few sips while looking at my phone, wishing it to make a message pop up from Ming. But no such luck.

"That's all you're going to have for breakfast," asks my mom.

"I'm not that hungry."

I don't tell my mom what happened because I don't feel like her trying to fix it.

"Don't worry, Mama, I'll make sure I eat when I get home. I'm not coming straight in because there are two women who want their nails done today."

"Okay, well, be careful out there," she says, smiling.

I give my mom a tight hug and a soft peck on her cheek. Even though my mom doesn't know about my status yet, I adore her and sometimes I just want to sit down and tell her, but I don't know how she will take it.

When something is bothering her, she usually needs someone to talk to and since it's a secret, I'll wait awhile before telling her.

"Love you, Mama."

"I love you too, sweetheart."

I grab my waist purse and put it around me while walking out the door and my mom locking up behind me.

***

"Good afternoon, Yvonne," says Dr. Grant as she is entering the exam room. "How have you been?"

"I've been better. I'm taking these new drugs on time every day and the side effects are slowly going away, but I still have vivid dreams and nightmares."

"That can be the side effects of your HIV regimen or from your antidepressants. Most patients continue their regimen unless it is too much to deal with. If this becomes an issue for you, please make sure you tell me. I must remind you that there aren't many regimens I can change for you because you've stopped taking your medicine during your early years of being in a state of denial. So, for you, changing drugs is an issue."

I nod. When I found out about my HIV. I went to many clinics to make sure the tests were correct. That's how bad I was in denial.

"So please make sure you continue with the ones you are taking now because we want you healthy and to continue being undetectable," she says.

"I have labs today, right?"

"Yes, but before you go, do you have any more questions for me," she asks.

"Well, you said you can't change my HIV regimen, but what about my antidepressant?"

"I have been trying to get you to talk to someone for a while now, but you refuse. I would like for you to see someone before I change your medication."

"I just don't see the point in getting a therapist," I say with a hard eye-roll. "Unless there is a cure for this virus in that session, talking will not help me. It will just depress me more."

"I can't make you, but if you change your mind, I can help set something up for you," says Dr. Grant, "and I'd rather you see a psychiatrist than a therapist."

I nod and leave for the lab room. I wasn't bullshitting. A therapist can't help me, and neither can a psychiatrist, although the latter can prescribe better meds. I know that the only way they can truly help me when it comes to my depression is for me to accept my status, and I know that I never will.

***

I am at my first client's house to do her nails, and she is running late. The rain stops and lucky for me since I'm stuck outside waiting. I send Thomas a message to at least look like I'm busy while I'm standing in front of this woman's building.

"Hi Thomas. I'm waiting for a late client, and I'm bored, so I thought of sending you a message. I hope you are doing okay."

Not much of an interesting message, but it's all I got. I look up at the cloudy sky and sigh. Please don't rain again, not now.

Thomas sends a reply: *"If I were in Chicago, I would pick you up and take you with me."*

Wait, what? If he could pick me up, I might've canceled on my clients. Okay, that's not right. They will have to understand. I laugh to myself at the thought of me hanging out with Thomas. What is he like? What would we do? I imagine him showing me around different areas and talking a lot about work. I often wonder how he is away from the screen. He seems cool when we chat, if I can get him to say more than a few words, but what is he really like? A trip would be nice if I were with him, but there is also the possibility of it being a joke.

I reply: *"You would? I wish. It would be nice to go somewhere different and get a change of scenery. How is your day so far? Is it sunny where you are?"*

Thomas replies: *"It's beautiful here in L. A. Since you seem to need a fresh change, it could be good for you. I'm guessing you haven't been here?"*

I reply: *"No. I have been to Hammond, Indiana, but that's close to me. A friend of mine lives there, but the more exciting places, I have not."*

Thomas replies: *"It's a tremendous difference from Chicago. You would enjoy it."*

I see my client running towards me from down the block. When she reaches me, she is catching her breath while trying to speak. She has on her pajamas with rollers still in her hair. I look her up and down, wondering where the hell did she go that she didn't have time to get dressed?

"Hey, Vonne! I'm so sorry I'm late. My bus driver acted like he was too scared to drive with his slow ass," Jade says.

"It's okay, I'm in the middle of a conversation anyway, you're good."

We head inside her building and up to the third floor. Felt more like the fifth. I really need to get in shape. Once inside her apartment, I see a pile of clothes on her sofa and a plethora of kid toys everywhere. She clears a seat for me and once seated, I finish my conversation with Thomas. Her ass is late anyway.

I reply: *"Maybe one day. I'm afraid to fly."*

Thomas replies: *"It's nothing to it. Maybe one day we can come here together. You'll see that flying is not as scary as you think."*

I send: *"Do you have family in Chicago?"*

Thomas answers: *"I do. A son and two daughters, along with my mother. My oldest daughter is in Lincoln Park while my mom, son, and other daughter are close to one another in Oak Park. I'm out in Country Club Hills but I spend a lot of time in L. A."*

I reply: *"Wow, were you born here? You know what? Save it for the next time we chat. My client is here. Can I message you later?"*

Thomas replies: *"Go on and handle that. Stay well."*

We end the chat with Thomas, sending the 'thumps up' emoji. I'm thinking when he sends emojis it's time to end the chat, even though I was the one who ended it this time. Well, he had more than 2 words to say this chat session. Mostly, we tell each other to stay well and good morning and night daily. His chats are short, but I like them. They kinda make my day.

***

After a long day of doing nails and thinking about if I should see a psychiatrist or not during the long bus ride home, all I can think of is food, a hot shower, and my bed.

When I walk in the door, my phone rings, and its Cashmere. By this time, I'm ready to have a nice brief discussion with her, but not before dinner. I press ignore.

"How was your doctor's visit," my mom asks.

I sigh deeply. "It was going great until she started bringing up a psychiatrist again."

She walks over to me and places her hands on my shoulders, ". If not, stop."

"I'll think about it, Mom. I promise."

After hugging her tightly, I ask, "So, where is dinner?"

"I left your plate on the stove. Just heat it in the microwave."

I can't help but to think about the conversation I had with Thomas today. He was more engaging than usual. I only know what he tells me, but he seems like a real down-to-earth guy. Maybe because he is just getting recognized and once he makes it big, he will turn into an asshole. God, I hope not.

Full and comfortable, I'm now ready to get into Cashmere's ass about Saturday. Soon as I pull out my phone to call her, she is calling me.

"Yup," I answer angrily.

"Listen, I did not mean for it to go the way that it did. I wanted to understand why you two seem to shut me and Karma out."

"You shouldn't have pushed! I hope you haven't been bugging her with calls like you were doing me after what the hell you did!"

I put the phone down to hear what my mom is doing. I'm pretty loud, but she is downstairs laughing at a television show. So, I put the phone back to my ear and lower my voice.

"I am so pissed at you," I say in an angry whisper.

"I will fix it. I'm really sorry. It's not that huge of a deal, is it?"

I hear her laugh nervously. Or is she just laughing?

"It's not funny." I can feel a headache coming on from how angry I am getting. "That's your problem, Cash."

"I'm not trying to be funny. I--," she tries to explain, but I'm done and end the call.

I'm wondering why Ming is ignoring my calls and texts. I've done nothing wrong. We are in the same boat here. Why won't she answer me? I lay down on my bed and think about how hurt and angry Ming must be. Do we really need Cash in our circle? She has always been pushy ever since I can remember, sometimes condescending. I think this time she has gone too far because Ming was almost pressured enough to spill the beans right in that crowded coffee shop.

***

It is now Tuesday morning and still not a word from Ming. I decide I'm going to pop up at her house because I'm worried, but then hear the doorbell. Could it be Ming? I race downstairs, get to the door, which seems like it has a boatload of locks. I can't get the door open fast enough just to see it's only Karma standing on my porch.

"Yvonne," she starts, "no one has heard from Ming. Not even her parents."

As I fall to the floor at the doorway into a squat position, my hands feel heavy as they struggle to hold my head. I am so frustrated! I try to think of a place that she can be but can't think of anything. I'm upset too, because Cash tries to get me dates and push, but I'm not that mad about it. Maybe it hits Ming differently. Just wish I knew where she is.

I rise and sigh deeply, "Come on in, Karma."

We both sit down on the sofa in silence.

"Maybe we should check the hospitals," Karma starts. "She left the coffee shop upset, and she was driving pretty erratic."

I'm rubbing the temples of my head in frustration, "If there were an accident, we would see it on the news or there would be phone calls."

There is another person at the door. Maybe my mom has a package coming. Or what if it's Cashmere? It better not be. I sigh heavily as I get up to see who it is.

There, standing on my porch, is Ming. She looks like she has been crying for days. Her hair looks like it hasn't been combed and she won't even look at me. I pull her into the tightest hug I have ever given to someone. I don't scold her for going M.I.A., I just hold her. We pull apart and her face turns to disgust. I forgot Karma is here just that quick. Ming turns around to leave, and I quickly take her hand.

"Cash isn't here," I say to Ming softly as I pull her inside, "I lit her ass up on the phone, trust me she wouldn't dare come over here right now."

Ming's resisting stops and she allows me to direct her to the sofa where Karma is already sitting.

"I am so glad to see you," I say. "I was so worried. You have to call one of us. Even if it's to say you are okay and to leave you alone. Just let us know you're ok, Ming."

Okay, I know I wasn't mad at her before. I think it just all came out when I saw she wasn't harmed. I mean, even her parents haven't seen her. She sits quietly and doesn't even look at us. What's on her mind? I wonder if she ran into Cash already and there is a murder scene we don't know about.

"Do you two want anything? I have--," then I'm suddenly cutoff by Ming.

"We don't need Cash," she says in a low voice.

"What," I and Karma exclaim simultaneously.

"I don't like that shit she pulled," says Ming, as her voice is becoming louder now. "We can do without her!"

"She is our friend. We can't just turn her away," Karma says. "You and Cash should sit down and talk when you're calm. This is the anger talking."

"No! There is nothing to talk about," Ming yells. "She should learn to stay in her own damn lane when it comes to people's issues. She can't just force someone to open up!"

"Ladies, please try to stay calm," I plead. "Karma is right. You should tell her how you feel and let her know she can't ever do that again, but do it when you are ready."

"Please, Ming," Karma begs.

Sighing deeply, Ming gives in. "Alright, I will talk to her, but it won't be right now. I'm still pissed."

Both Karma and I look as if we are both thanking the gods as we breathe a vast sigh of relief.

"Well," Ming starts as she's getting up from the sofa, "I'm going to head home to clear my head and relax before work tomorrow. I can't cancel any more clients."

"Sure," I say as I stand. "I am so happy to see you and that you're ok. The scare you gave me."

I playfully shove Ming, and we both smile.

"I'm sorry you two," she says, "I just wanted to be alone after all of that."

"I am going to head out too," Karma says while smiling nervously. "I'm glad to see you both."

We all hug, and I tell them both to drive safely before closing the door and locking it.

I have the house to myself since my mom went to stay a week with her younger sister. I can't help but wonder how the conversation is going to go between Cashmere and Ming. We have had disagreements before, but not like this, where one of us is considering ending a friendship.

***

The sun is still burning hot and is incredibly bright out even at 7:00 pm. I grab my tablet and take it out to the backyard to start another conversation with Thomas. They are usually short, but I am hoping it's long enough to keep my mind off the meeting that will happen between my two friends.

"Hi Thomas. I hope your day is going way better than mine." I end it with a 'smile' emoji.

I see a meme that I think is funny in my 'MediaPal' feed and send it to him. It says, "I refuse to let the conversation die if I really like you. I'll start asking shit like "Do you like neck bones?"

We have chatted a while, but most were "hi and hope you're well" texts. There is a woman that also follows his page that keeps his attention. She is another fan as far as I can tell, but she gets "I love you's" and 'heart' emojis. I'm almost jealous. Well, he said he would bring me to Los Angeles, but I think he's only kidding. We once chatted about his projects, and he seems so excited about them. Hmm, I guess we do chat. Okay, maybe I am being greedy and want him to keep the conversation going longer. Sue me, okay! I send the meme because I think it's silly and harmless.

I sit out a few more hours playing games on my tablet. The sun is going down and I head inside to shower and relax. It's too hot to cook, even with the air conditioning on.

I pick up a menu on the table that my mom left out when she was here. Chinese? Maybe a chicken meal. I cannot decide. Instead, I look in the freezer to see if we have any quick meals and there is a chicken pot pie box staring at me. I grab that, pop it in the microwave, and I look at the message. Nothing yet from Thomas. Eating dinner alone. Yes, this is my life in my late 30s.

I wonder if this is how my life is going to be? I mean yeah; I talk to guys all the time, but I sure as hell know that not one guy is going to be with me while I have this virus. Haven't thought about it in years, about where I got it from? I was not promiscuous, nor did any drugs. When I watch movies, read articles or forums about how one might catch HIV, it's always the "she must have been a ho" or "maybe it was from a gay relationship." I read that men who are gay would marry straight women to keep their secret of them being gay and then pass the virus to their wives. How did I get mine? Did an undercover gay guy do that to me? I can feel myself becoming depressed at these thoughts. So yeah, brain, it's time to change the subject.

My phone pings and as I look at the message, I can't believe what I am reading. Thomas sends a message back, and he doesn't seem happy at all.

"Look, 'Vonne Vonne'," (He goes by my profile handle. Probably never even paid any attention to my name

when I gave it anyway.) *"You seem like a sweet young woman, but I don't communicate through social media much and I have a lot going on,"* (But you said at the beginning that you do communicate in direct messages, but please go on) *"I don't answer messages right away because I have a busy schedule which I remember telling you. I am working on many things."*

I'm thinking he thinks I want a quick response. I don't care when he responds. I was only joking about how he isn't interacting with me much. He was acting differently. I mean, he chats, but not really. After we chatted while I waited for my client, Thomas started not answering me or would read my messages and not say anything. If he answered, the messages were brief, and it seems like he did a complete 180 on me.

I reply: *"I did not mean for the meme to offend you. I know you're busy. Just thought the meme was a little funny and that we would both laugh about it. It was not for you to rush and answer. I was joking because you are so limited when it comes to conversation. I apologize."*

I know that sometimes it's hard to know a person's tone when reading a text from them, but I almost feel like I annoyed him just now. I wonder a lot if he wants me to stop. He is a grown man. I'm sure if he wants me to, he would just say so. He isn't the same. Something's off.

He replies: *"You're fine. You, my love, can do no wrong."* Then a 'heart,' emoji.

I read his reply and I can feel my cheeks expanding. I am really blushing, but I don't want to keep him, so I type good night and he types the same and I leave it at that. Sometimes he confuses me. I hate rejection so I never want to ask to meet even though he said he would take me to L.A. I fear I may be reading into this whole situation wrong and If I am, I would be so embarrassed that I may shutdown all social media and wallow in my stupidity.

My phone rings, and it's Karma. I'm thinking out loud, "What now?"

"Hey, Karma, what's going on," I ask.

"Well, Ming wants everyone to meet at her house tomorrow evening," she says. "Will you be able to make it?"

Usually, I don't want to go out on short notice, but something tells me I should.

"Yeah, I'll be there," I answer. "I should get there around 6."

"I can come pick you up," Karma offers.

All my friends are driving, but me. They live on the north side of the city. I learned to drive but I am afraid to. People are always in a hurry and the last thing I want is to be in an accident I caused because of anxiety. I am such a scary bitch.

"No, you don't have to come all the way here and then go back. I'll be there, girl. Don't worry."

I want to message Thomas some more, but; I remember in some of his messages that I haven't been thinking about is he has a new gig that he is starring in but didn't want to share with me yet, so I will leave him be for now. Okay, maybe I will just wait on him to reach out to me instead, since he made it abundantly clear how busy he is.

Thomas looks really good for his age. He is 57 and could pass for mid to late thirties, maybe. He told me he has family in Chicago, and he lives in Country Club Hills, a Chicago suburb. We joke here and there. I would flirt with him a little, but Thomas, well, he seems to joke with me, but I don't think he was flirting back. He is more focused on his job, or maybe his interests are elsewhere.

I look at the clock and I say aloud, "Okay, Yvonne. That is enough daydreaming. Have to get ready to get to Ming's and see what the hell is going on now."

It's almost 2 pm and since I'm on public transportation, I know I have to make sure that I am ready so I can leave at a good time to be at Ming's tonight. Traveling on the bus is a bitch sometimes, with the scheduling, the arrival times and all of that. I really need to think about a car. Seriously.

I look in the mirror at myself to check my appearance. I decide to wear my naturally curly shoulder-length hair with the part down the center. My makeup is fine. I put on my waist purse, look at messages on my phone before putting it away, grab my keys, and I'm off.

***

"Ugh! Here comes trouble," I say with a heavy sigh and rolling my eyes.

I can see Cashmere walking down the street from the building next to Ming's, also going to her house as I step off the bus. We meet right at the gate entrance of the building.

"What's up, Chica," Cashmere says with a light laugh.

I roll my eyes at her and open the gate to go inside. I hear her laugh as she follows close behind me.

They still have not fixed the building's door, so there is no need to ring the bell as we both walk upstairs. I knock and Ming opens the door. I mutter "incoming" as I go inside.

Ming steps back to let Cashmere inside the apartment, then closes the door.

"Thank you all for coming."

Karma is here already. She is sitting on the sofa snacking on a small bag of chips. Cashmere and I go to our seats while Ming continues to stand.

"As you all know," Ming begins, "I have been keeping my distance since that Saturday night at Rita's coffee shop, but now there are some things that I want to get off my chest."

Karma shifts in her seat as if she is nervous or trying to get comfortable.

"I don't know what the issue is," Cashmere butts in, "I just wanted to know why you and Yvonne are so antisocial when it comes to me and Karma?"

I shake my head because I know it is about to go down now. I then look at Cashmere with an expression on my face, as I mouth the words "shut the hell up"!

"Don't interrupt me," Ming yells.

"Sorry, Jeez," Cashmere snaps, who then folds her arms like a pouty child.

"I want to start by saying that I dislike how you attacked me and Yvonne at the coffee shop," Ming says calmly. "If I am not ready to talk about something with you, then I am not ready and I will do so in my own time."

Ming sits down in a chair near Cashmere. I hold my breath as she sits thinking she may hit her or something, but she just sits and gives her a daunting stare.

"You can't push people, Cashmere. Yes, we are friends, but that does not mean that you push and push until you get your way. I was so upset that I was going to never speak to you again, but the ladies have convinced me to talk it out. So here we are."

Cashmere clears her throat, then chuckles. "Well, I apologize for how I attacked and pushed at the shop. Just so tired of you and Yvonne acting as if me and Karma are strangers. But after how you acted, it won't happen again."

Oh, shit.

"What the hell do you mean, how I acted," Ming yells as she rises from her seat. "I had every right to act how I did. You did that in a public place, and you know how private I am."

"I said I'm sorry," Cashmere yells back. "Jeez, everyone is so damn sensitive around here!"

This was getting worse quickly. Karma sits with a chip on its way to her mouth but stops short. I am getting nervous. I have to step in.

"Can I just say something," I ask while sitting up in my seat.

"Go ahead, Vonne," Ming says while lowering her voice. "Better you than this bit—. "

"Whoa," I cut in. "Okay everyone, just calm down."

I am going to try my best in reasoning with them and hopefully, they will get back on good terms. Poor Karma looks scared. I know she doesn't want the friendship to end, but if this isn't fixed tonight, we will be divided.

"Listen," I start, "we are all friends and have been for a very long time. We have had our issues, and this one is no different. It is an issue. We just need to work through it like we always do."

Cashmere looks down at her hands and Ming is still looking like she could kill someone. Karma is just quiet, looking on at everything while snacking.

"Cash, Ming is saying that even though you two are friends, there is no need to press her to tell you what is on her mind or what's going on. She will come to you for help on her own time, but she is still a friend. She just wants to deal with it her way first."

Cashmere sighs softly. I know she wants us all to act like friends. With me not wanting to come out of the house and Ming wanting to work her issues privately, no wonder Cash feels the group is a bit divided.

"Ming," I say, "Cash is just worried, and she is pushing because maybe she feels as if she can help in some way. So, please don't be angry with her. You both just need to respect each other's space and if one of us says that we aren't ready to talk about what is wrong, then we should respect it."

"Alright, alright," Cashmere says.

She is looking more serious now. I can tell that she is a tad bit upset cause she didn't get her way. It's time the learns to stop forcing shit with us.

"I apologize, Ming. At first, I didn't think that it was hurting anyone, but now I see how upset it made you. Maybe it's time I slow down. I also want to apologize to you too, Yvonne. It won't happen again."

Well, at least she looks apologetic this time. So maybe Ming and Cashmere's friendship can be saved. I give it until next week until Cash fucks up again. I think Ming is going through something and it's making her more sensitive to things. If she is, my guess is she will come to me first to talk about it before she goes anywhere near Cash or Karma.

"Thank you, Cash," Ming says while walking towards a still seated Cashmere, leans down and embraces her. "That means a lot. When I'm ready, I will sit down with you. You're still my friend, so don't think because I have not confided in you yet means that we are not, because we are."

"Now that's what I'm talking about," Karma says, joining in on the hug.

I join in too. Here we are, all hugging it out like we always do when we have an issue. It feels so good now we can put that behind us and hopefully Cashmere will be on her best behavior because she is always just "trying to help" as she says.

"I need to go if I want to get home while the buses are running," I say as I separate from the ladies.

If I were thinking I would have brought my drugs with me and now I have to figure out how to get out of staying the night because I can't miss a day of the medicine.

"But it will be after midnight by the time you get home," Ming says, "Stay here tonight."

"I'll be fine, " I say while gathering my things, "I forgot to bring my meds."

"For your depression," asks Cashmere.

We'll go with that which is what I say in my mind, but what I say is, "Yes, I forgot my antidepressant. Talk to you all later."

I give more hugs before rushing out to catch my bus.

3

Blood Connection

It's a beautiful fall morning. My friends have had their talk and seem to be doing fine, even a month later. There is a couple's fair coming and I still don't have a date and I don't think Ming has one either. I want us all to go this year, so I'm thinking of asking someone to go with. A date to the fair and nothing else, only to show face and be there without feeling awkward because I'm alone. The fair is 3 days from now, so I need to find my date and fast.

I am meeting Ming downtown this afternoon so that we can shop. Well, I will be "wish shopping" because I get funds monthly and I have a little over a week before I collect my disability check.

"What you doing today, sweetie," my mom asks.

"Going to meet Ming in a little while," I answer.

"It's been over a month. Have you seen a therapist or psychiatrist yet?"

I have not seen one and I wish my mom would stop asking me, but maybe she's right. A therapist may do me some good. I think I'll try a therapist first to see how I do. Psychiatrist sound so intimidating. Ugh! I'm just not ready to spill my secrets to a complete stranger.

"Nope, not yet. I will, Mama, don't worry."

She looks at me and before she opens her mouth to protest, I grab my things.

"I need to get going. I love you," I say, walking towards the door.

My mom frowns. "Mhm, we will talk about this when you get back. I mean it."

***

"Ming," I yell, while heading in her direction.

"Hi, Vonne," she greets, then sips her coffee. "I don't know why we are shopping; we never go to the couple's fair."

"I think we should all go," I say, while looking around at the different stores in our vicinity. "I know I'm usually at home, but I am trying to get out there again."

Ming looks at me as if she doesn't believe what I have just said.

"Really? Why the sudden change," she asks.

I look to the ground, then back to her.

"I'm 37 years old, Ming, I'm still in good shape, healthy and I don't want to waste away sitting at home because of my health."

My eyes are filling with tears. With crowds of people passing by, I look away.

"I know there is no one that will be with me, so I guess I'm learning to live with that. Staying in the house will not cure me. It only keeps me discreet from people that I hope have forgotten who I am. I don't want anyone to know. It depresses me when waking up every day and I have a ton of meds to take and think about being alone for the rest of my life. You are going through the same thing. Don't you ever feel like you can't be alone?"

"Oh Vonnie."

"No, Ming, it's true. Thomas will never be with me. No man will. I'm fine with that. I have to be."

Tears are falling down my cheeks, and I can't hold them back. Ming tries consoling me, but to no avail.

"You notice why I haven't talked about Thomas much," I ask Ming.

We are still at the meeting point downtown, the park at the bus stop on Balbo and Michigan. I sit down on the nearest bench and Ming joins me.

I have not told her that at the end of the summer, Thomas and I had a conversation. After Ming and Cashmere made up, I left. I got home to start a chat with Thomas like I sometimes do, and he was very distant. He wanted to meet and go for coffee before he left for L.A., again, and I was fine with that. Before that day came, we had chat more about work and different things happening with us and then he asked if I was dating.

ThomasEg: *"You are a beautiful young woman and seem very nice. I find it hard to believe that you aren't seeing anyone."*

VonneVonne: *"Well, it's a very long story. I may tell it one day."*

ThomasEg: *"Let me guess, your heart was broken and now you hate all men?"* *'Laughing,' emoji.*

VonneVonne: *"Someone has hurt me before, but this is ten times worse."*

I want so much to tell this guy that I'm so damaged but fear he will no longer be interested in me. We are flirting back and forth in this messenger app, (well, I am not sure about him) and I want to keep it going. Am I wrong for not being upfront?

ThomasEg: *"Yvonne, I feel there is something you want to tell me."*

"There is, Thomas," I type as I fight to hold back tears. "I am living with HIV! I am HIV positive!"

There is a long pause, and I can't take it anymore. I slam my laptop shut, leaving Thomas with his thoughts of what I have just revealed about me. I get up from the desk sobbing, and storm into my bed, lay in a fetal position, and cry until I fall asleep.

Back downtown where I am with Ming, I look at her after telling her what happened with Thomas, and her eyes are wide and jaw nearly to the ground.

"Oh my God, you told him," Ming exclaims.

I nod as I'm wiping my tears.

"I did."

"Well, did he ever get back to you?"

"No, not yet, and I don't think he will. He is still following me on 'MediaPal', but not a word since the end of the summer."

She scoots over to hug me, and I sit and cry until I can't anymore.

"Enough about that," I say with a slight chuckle. "We have some shopping to do, and I need to find someone that will go with me to this fair."

"I have someone to go with me and I may have someone for you too," says Ming.

"You have a date?"

"I know, right," says Ming while she giggles. "Hell has frozen over."

"I'm thrilled for you, Ming," I say with a smile. "You really need this."

"Let's go get our outfits before we flood downtown with our tears," Ming says.

She rises, then grabs my hand and pulls me off the park bench. We both walk into a small department store. I look around and walk up to a halter top pantsuit. My eyes stretch wide open as I see the price tag. This store is not for my poor ass.

"I'll be 'wish shopping' for real," I mutter.

"What's that, Vonnie," Ming asks while looking at a few tops near the cash register.

"Oh nothing," I answer.

We are the only two in the small store. Most of the items look vintage. Fits Ming's tastes. I see a pair of jeans with a boho top and decide nothing in this shop is for me and find a seat near the dressing rooms.

"Listen, there is something I should tell you, Vonnie."

I look over at Ming.

"What is it?"

"I'll tell you on the drive to your house when we're done shopping," she says.

We go to a few stores, stop for coffee, laugh, and talk the whole afternoon. I finally find something that I can afford at the fourth store. A maxi skirt, brown with a short sleeve top that is light tan with fall leaves right at the entrance. It's perfect!

"Are you getting that," Ming asks, looking over my shoulder.

"I like it. I think it fits the season."

She collects the articles of clothing off the rack after forcing me to say my size and walks it over to the counter.

"Ming, thanks, but I can pay," I say as I follow behind her.

Ming objects and continues pulling her credit card out of her purse. "I know you can, but its fine. I got it."

Seeing that I'm being gifted, I just look on at Ming and the cashier's interaction. I guess I can use the money to get my hair done.

"Thanks, Ming," I say as I grab the bag off the counter, "I'll pay you back."

She laughs and rolls her eyes. "Girl, if you don't stop!"

***

On our way to my house, the rush hour ride is full of us stopping and going every two seconds. Ming seems happy, so I'm guessing that what she wants to talk about isn't too bad.

"So, what was it you wanted to tell me," I ask Ming.

"Nothing bad," she says with a chuckle. "I just wanna tell you about Jesse."

"The guy that you're seeing," I ask.

"Yeah. I have known him for a few years now."

"Wait, you kept this even from me? I'm not upset or--."

Ming cuts me off. "I didn't tell you because you have been wanting someone to love and for them to love you, too. I have only been seeing Jesse for a week after running into him at work."

"He is a client? I thought you can't date your clients."

"I can't. I sent him to another colleague. He is the one that infected me, Vonnie."

My jaw drops. I am thinking this man has infected you with HIV and now you want to date him? How can she? If it were me, I would still be furious. I won't question it since she's giving me the info anyway, and I don't want her to regret opening up to me about it. So, I say nothing.

"I was at a low point in my life a few years back and I ended up using," Ming says. "I shared a needle with Jesse, and it wasn't just one time. There were a few times we used together."

"Ming... you could have come to me before... taking that route!"

What the hell am I saying? As damaged as I am, I would have joined them in the feeling of being numb, injecting my thoughts, pain, and life away.

"Oh please, Vonne," Ming says while she sighs heavily with eye rolls, "you are going through just as much as I am, if not more. You probably would have brought your own damn needle."

I can't help but laugh. Still, I would rather her come and talk to me than hurting her body. Drug use is so harmful, and most don't come back from it.

"I just mean that maybe it would have helped you to confide in me what was happening, but you got a guy out of it, and you look happy," I say while grinning.

"Yeah, I guess you're right. I'm just scared to introduce him to Cash and Karma," Ming says with her face changing from happy to worry. "I know Cash will have a lot of questions."

"Is he discreet about his status," I ask.

"No, not really, and that's the problem, but our connection is so good that I'm willing to overlook that part. I do plan on talking to him about it because I am not as open about my status as he is."

"A connection by blood," I say mistakenly out loud, but actually thinking it.

"You are not funny," Ming says while laughing.

I join in on her laughter as I say, "I hope it works out".

"We're here," Ming says as she pulls up to my house.

"It looks dark. Maybe my mom is asleep early. Thanks for everything. Call me when you get home, please."

I get out of the car and when I reach the top step, turn to wave Ming off, watching as she drives away.

Once inside, I see the house is dark, like I thought. I look around the house, and my mom is nowhere to be found.

"Mom," I call out, "are you here?"

She comes out of the bathroom.

"Oh, hey sweetie," my mom says while coming out of the bathroom and fanning the air. "Hope you don't have to go in there."

My mom finds air freshener and sprays a heavy amount of aerosol throughout the house.

"Mom, that's enough," I shout, while taking the spray out of her hand. "You trying to kill us?"

"I'm trying to save your nose," she laughs. "I didn't cook tonight, couldn't stay out of the bathroom."

I sit the aerosol can down on the side table, giving my mom a stern look.

"Don't worry, I'll make something. Just please stay away from that spray?"

Cook? I'll order something. I'm tired and I don't feel like cooking a meal tonight. I sit down at the kitchen table, pull out my phone, to look through the food app menu. No, I want to message Thomas first, so I find the 'MediaPal' app and Thomas' account.

VonneVonne: *"Thomas?"*

That was all I could come up with. I had told the man about my HIV status and I'm sure he has me muted by now. I go back to the message and see that he has read it. So, I leave another one.

VonneVonne: *"If you don't want me to message you again, just say not to! Don't just read the messages and say nothing. I know you are ignoring me because of what I told you."*

Why do I even care? I knew this was the response I'd get. It still hurts. I miss the Thomas that joked, messaged, and checked on me. Now, I think I lost him, and I only initially just loved the chats. I wasn't looking to date. His messages alone made my day. Now I've fallen for him and can't even be with anyone.

ThomasEg: *"Listen, I have a lot going on with fitness and work. One day we will get to chat, but it can't be right now because I am very busy."*

My heart sinks. I know that last message means he isn't going to message me much anymore, or at all. I don't bother responding. Just like the other guys I tried to be upfront with, I get the same response. It is time for me to just accept the loss of what could have been a friendship. I close the app, trying not to cry, and I don't have an appetite anymore, so I put in an order of chicken and potato wedges for my mom. I will not be eating tonight.

***

I wake up feeling sad from last night. Thomas is no longer responding to my direct messages or reacting to anything that I post.. What I don't understand is why is he still following me? Why not delete or even block me? I could tell that today was going to be one of those days that I am sad all day and don't want to be bothered.

I'm happy for Ming, though. She was smiling, glowing, and so happy. I'm the only one in the group single now and finding a date went downhill after last night. I was not going to the fair this year because now I am not in the mood to.

Since I'm going to be indoors for a few days, I plan everything I want to do. I sit out all my nail polishes, files, led lamp, and the forms. I figure I'll just spend the day at home doing my nails. Maybe give myself a facial and change my hair color. I don't know why I suddenly want to do these things, but that is what I am going to do today.

Then, all that energy goes away. I am so down that I just want to get back in bed and sleep my Saturday away. I keep looking at my phone as if Thomas left me a message, and I somehow missed it. Nothing there.

I look to see who is texting me. It's my mom asking if I want anything to eat. I send her a message back saying no and that I am going to sleep in today. I don't want to worry her, and I don't want her questioning me, either.

For me to want love in my life, sometimes I don't want it at all. I go through Thomas' profile and see all the beautiful women he follows. It makes me think about all I see are people lusting after each other. I've lusted too. I still want that love with someone that has a strong, unbreakable bond but doesn't see that happening. People nowadays cheat at a drop of a hat. Men seem to be more interested in the fake bodies than a woman like me who works out almost every day and watches what I eat to keep this bangin' body I have naturally.

As my brain is active with depressing thoughts on love, my phone rings. I answer and its Karma. I know she's calling about the fair that's coming up. Should've just let it ring.

"Hey, Karma."

"Hey, girl! I'm calling to let you know they are going to move the fair for this upcoming Saturday."

Great! A week for my friends to try to change my mind into going once I tell them I'm not.

"Yay," I say, so notably unenthused.

"Listen, I know you hate going, but Ming said she bought you an outfit.

"I still have my receipt."

It's Sunday night now, so I have 6 days to decide if I am going or not. I still choose the latter.

"I just don't feel well," I add. "I'll go next year. Besides, we have an entire week, and I may feel better later."

There is silence, then a heavy sigh from Karma, who I know is going right back to the girls with my decision. I roll my eyes at that thought.

"Okay, Vonne, just let us know if you change your mind. Whatever it is, I hope you feel better."

"Thanks."

We say our goodbyes and hang up.

***

I wake up Monday morning and I try not to look at Thomas' profile, but I can't help it. No new messages. After becoming nosy and seeing the beautiful women he follows, mostly white or very light-skinned, I am thinking maybe he does not like black women at all. Maybe he was just being nice to me because I am a fan. What if it isn't HIV, he is afraid of, and I'm just not his type because I have more melanin than the women he is following? Laughing at that thought, I roll my eyes. Who am I kidding? It's the HIV. Anyway, I know if a guy has a certain type, there is no changing that. It seems fair skin is more desired for our black men and not just them, but other races, too. I'm getting more depressed by the minute thinking about this because here is a guy I'm crushing on, and he probably doesn't even like women with the same skin color as me. I really need a hobby. All I think about is his ass.

I wash my face, brush my teeth, and look outside my window. As I feel the sun's warm rays, I wonder if I even want to go out today. I need something to keep my mind from my sad life. In my room, there is a stack of books in the corner on the floor. Walking over, I pick up the first one of the enormous stacks to see that it's my pharmacy calculations. I could find a job. I used to work as a pharmacy technician, but mental illness was getting in the way. Being at home was helping me because I didn't enjoy leaving the house, but is it good for me? Going back to work may be a better option.

I walk over to my desk, sit in front of my computer, and contemplate on looking for job openings. My license for pharmacy technician clearly expired since I applied over 7 years ago.

"Yvonne," my mom yells from downstairs, "are you hungry?"

"Nah, but I may eat later."

I then think about what my mom said I should do. Talk to a therapist or psychiatrist. I'll start with a therapist first. A psychiatrist seems so serious, like I'm crazy or something. I switch from the job listings and instead look up therapists in my area. I come across a woman, white with a friendly face. Don't think I need a therapist since I have Ming, but perhaps I should reach out to those who aren't close to me and see how it is.

Ming is glowing, and I'd be lying if I said I don't envy her just a little. She has found someone, and it is so ironic that it is the very person who infected her with the HIV virus. A literal blood connection. That's how I see it after the story she has told me. A therapist may be someone who can help me love myself more in order for me to love someone truly and that person to return the love back to me. So, I decide to make an appointment.

Now that I have the appointment out of the way, my mom can get off my back and I can go to the store to cure my cravings for processed food. I'm feeling good about this appointment, and I never thought I would speak to a therapist. Time to reward myself. I throw on some leggings with an oversized top and head downstairs.

"Mom, I'm on my way out to the store. Want anything?"

"Yeah, some chips and an orange pop," she answers from the kitchen.

I grab what I need and leave. Usually, I get like this when I'm sad. Becoming a glutton for snacks and eat my problems away.

***

"Hey, Miss Sexy," says a guy sitting on his porch as I walk by, "wit cho fine ass."

I roll my eyes before looking over in his direction. I look at him and respond, "Hello, how are you?"

"I'm good now that you in my presence," he says with a smirk.

I want to say "Trust me, you don't want none of this" but he would only translate it as me being an uppity bitch and get angry, so why bother?

"Can I holla at you fo a sec," he asks before pulling a long drag of his half-done cigarette.

I know my English isn't all that great, but that is a turnoff when a guy approaches me with that 'hood' shit.

"No, I have a disabled mom at home waiting for me to get back from the store with the items she needs."

"I can walk--,"

I cut him off. I am not in the fucking mood for his persistence.

"Well, have a wonderful afternoon," I say with a smile as I keep walking hastily.

Men try to talk to me all the time, and I guess I am as picky as most. I still, however, love my black men, just not the type who sit on the porch smoking cigarettes with a beer in hand, wearing 'wife-beaters' all day, looking high as hell.

I finally made it to the tiny store and the regular Arab guy is there who flirts a lot, but I know it's not just me, it's all women who enter this place. He doesn't say much today, just gives me a smile with a wink.

***

Alcohol, processed foods, chips, soft drinks, and candies. This place is my pharmacy for depression and the way I am feeling right now, it's time for a refill.

Suddenly, a young skinny dark-skinned man with pants falling off his ass and no shirt rushes into the store with the Chicago detectives charging right behind him. This store is no bigger than the size of a small bedroom, making it easy for the detectives to corner their alleged suspect. During this process, I'm knocked down onto the filthy, sticky floor.

"We saw you sell to the undercover cop," one of them says to the young man with his hand on his gun, still in the holster.

"Yo ass ain't seen shit, muthafucka," the young man screams, then rushes toward them, trying to make his escape.

I'm on the floor looking on and thinking that I better not get shot over this. I have enough on my plate.

Both detectives grab the man as he tries to make his very unsuccessful getaway and throw him on the floor, cuffing him. Once the young man is on his feet, only one leads him to the car. The other looks at me on the floor and holds out his hand to help me up.

"Did I knock you down," he asks. "I apologize."

He looks at me and smiles.

"Thanks," I say, looking away to keep him from seeing me blush.

I dust myself off. The floor looks like someone has not mopped it in ages. After thoughts of me in a bleach bath, I look back to the detective. He is a white guy, very attractive with a full beard, tall, muscular build, and a lot of tattoos.

We both look towards the exit where we can hear his partner and their alleged suspect screaming obscenities to one another.

The detective pulls out a small notepad and starts scribbling, "Hey, I can't stay long. Here's my number. My name is Jason. Call me later tonight."

He hands me the folded-up paper that has his info on it, and I take it. We both look at each other and smile. Then he runs out of the messy store that's now in disarray from the scuffle that happened a few moments earlier. I watch them drive away and I left shortly after, not buying a thing with everything all over the place. I can hear the store owner swearing, which is my guess, in Arabic over the damages.

I can feel myself smiling as I walk home and then I remember to go around the block, so I don't walk past the "porch guy" I encountered earlier. Soon as my mind races, my smile is short-lived. If I decide to call the detective later tonight, do I tell him my status right away? No. Not this time. I'm going to wait and see where it goes. I'm not saying a word until the time is right. That is what I decide.

There is one problem though, and that is I still have feelings for Thomas, and we have not even met. No matter, I am still going to call Jason tonight. Thomas and I have chatted for about 4 months and it seems he isn't interested. Maybe it is time for me to fall back. He may not even notice I have left him alone. I was never that important to him, anyway. Just another fan that he could chat with for a short while.

I enter my house smiling except I wasn't aware I started smiling again until my mom points it out.

"What are you smiling about," my mom asks while smiling with me. "Whatever have you so happy made you forget about my junk food I see."

"No, Mom. There was an incident at the store up the street."

"What?!"

"Don't worry, Mama. The detectives got the guy, and no one was hurt. Well, the store owner wasn't too happy with a wrecked place."

"Then what were you smiling about when you came in?"

"One detective gave me his number. He is a good-looking, a white man."

"A white man," she asks with eyebrows raised, "and a cop at that."

"Mom, please stop."

"I'm sorry, but you know I don't trust them," my mom says while walking away, "but you grown, so it's your business."

"I can go to another store if you want."

Something tells me that after I told her that a white man has given me his number, she's not interested in snacks anymore.

"Don't worry about it, sweetie. All it means is we didn't need that mess in our bodies, anyway."

***

It's almost 8 pm and I decide to try the number Jason gave me. I listen to it ring and after the fourth, I hear a man on the other end.

"This is Jason," he answers.

There is a momentary pause.

"Um... hi... Jason. It's Yvonne... from the store on 106th St where you and your partner--. "

"Yes, I remember you," he interrupts. "I'm glad you called. I just got out the shower."

"I'm sorry. Do you want me to call back?"

"No, no, no. I honestly didn't think I would hear from you."

"Why is that?"

"I think you know the black community isn't very fond of the cops, particularly us white ones."

Well, he isn't lying. I didn't even think about it, though, until my mom mentioned it earlier.

"I don't want to judge without getting to know you. So, I'm glad that I called," I say with a smile. Not that he could see it, but I could hear him chuckling softly from his end.

"Tell you what, Yvonne. How about we meet up tomorrow afternoon for a cup of coffee? Does that sound good?"

"It sounds great!"

"1 pm good," he asks.

"1 pm is fine," I answer.

"See you then, beautiful."

After we hang up, I think to call Ming, but the last thing I want to do is jinx this. I feel so sure about this meeting, but I want to see him a few times before I mention anything about him to the others. If we click, he may be the person I take to the fair on Saturday.

I remember I made an appointment to see a therapist, and it's for tomorrow at 9 am. I hope I made the right choice in doing this. It's on the same day as my first coffee meet with Jason and it scares me. If the session goes bad, there is a chance I will ghost him.

I lay in bed with my phone going through my social media and I see Thomas interacting with everyone, but not with me like he used to. "Maybe he has muted me," I say to myself out loud. I can't really tell if I am muted or not, but I might be. I put my phone down and start thinking about Jason. How will this coffee date go? How will he react to my status when I decide to tell him?

I'm glad my mom is staying a week at my aunt's house, so I will have the house to myself if Jason and I decide to come here after having coffee. Tomorrow will be busy for me. I don't enjoy leaving the house and have two places to be. I try shutting my mind off so that I can be up in the morning for my first session. After a while, I feel myself drift off.

***

I open my eyes and I just lay there listening to the light traffic go up and down my street. Fifteen minutes later, I pick up my phone and see it's 830 am. That's no time to get ready! The session starts in 30 minutes. Wake up, Vonne, shit!

"Call Therapist," I yell at my phone.

The phone rings and a woman with a soft voice answer.

"Hi, thank you for calling Stoney Counseling, Doris speaking."

"Good morning, I'm Yvonne Dent and I have a 9 am appointment to see Bethany Wilkins, but I won't be able to make it because I'm just waking up."

"Oh no," Doris gasps lightly. "We can see you virtually if you have a webcam available."

"Yes, I have one here."

"Great," she says cheerfully. "Just a sec while I inform Bethany that you are on the line and would like the session virtually instead."

"Thanks!"

During this time, I'm throwing on a decent top and trying to fix my hair so that I'm presentable for the camera before Doris returns to the call.

"Okay, we are going to change the time to 10 this morning and sending you some things in the email that you used when you signed up with us. Is that email fine?"

"Yes, it is."

"Alright, sending the questionnaire over to you and you can fill out your insurance information and once done, send everything back in that email."

We hang up. Now I have time to dress properly, but what do I want to wear for the coffee date?

I decide to wear my fitted jeans, black leather ankle heel boots, with a crochet-knit top. My 3c soft curls will flow and fall freely. I apply natural makeup, mostly brown tones, brown lips, light brown shadow, and a light brown highlight.

"Almost time for my session," I say to myself out loud.

I sit down at my desk and use my last 15 minutes to send my questionnaire and insurance information back to Doris before turning on my camera and wait.

As I wait for the therapist, I look at 'MediaPal' and see a new post that Thomas shared of a popular show he will be joining. As I read it, I sigh. Great, now I have to watch a guy I'm trying not to think about, on one of my favorite shows. I knew it was happening. He mentioned it to me back when we were chatting this past summer. Now that it's certain, I'm not sure if I want to keep watching. Maybe Jason will be the man to keep Thomas out of my thoughts.

A woman, who looks to be in her early 60s, appears on my screen. You can tell that she covered her grays with the red dye job she has, and her face gives away her age.

"Good morning, Yvonne, or would you prefer Miss Dent?"

"Yvonne is fine," I say with a smile.

"Well, I'm Bethany, and it's nice to meet you. Yvonne, let's start by you telling me a little about yourself and then we can go from there. If you don't mind, I'd like to take notes during this session."

"Sure, I don't mind at all."

I don't know where to start. I want to do this because maybe it will be right for me and ever since I finally told my mom about my positive status at the end of this past summer, she kept pushing me to talk to someone. If I don't like it, I can stop.

"Well, I'm 37, single, no kids and at my age, I feel like my life is nothing. Like I am a waste."

I look to see her jotting everything that I say down in her notebook. So, guessing that I am doing okay, I continue.

"When I was 21 years old, I found out that I was HIV positive, and was living in denial for almost 12 years."

She stops writing and looks up to the screen at me.

"Is this why you feel like your life is a waste," she asks.

"Well, yes. You see, I cannot date without worrying about passing it on. I can't have children. When I try to date or live a normal life, any guy that I tell my status to cut me off and I never hear from them again. The stigma associated with this virus is unforgiving, I think, and as long as people look down on it, I'll never have a genuine friendship or a relationship."

"Yvonne, there are many people who are HIV positive that have husbands and children. The person who you may be attracted to may not want to be with you, but there are others."

"I find it hard to believe that HIV-positive people are in relationships with children. Are they dating other positive people?"

"On the contrary," she says, "in fact, there are a lot of negative people who are seeing positive people than you think. Do you know anything about the virus that you have?"

I know nothing about the virus, except that I didn't want it and my love life is shit because of it and that I am so ashamed I can't even tell my friends and family.

"I guess I don't. Just know I've been getting negative reactions because of the virus, and it's depressing and don't want to think about it. Hence is why I was in denial for so many years. I don't even know what my labs mean."

I feel myself getting emotional and I try to fight back my tears. Even upset, all I can think about is I really do not want to remove my makeup and start all over.

"I tried to be honest and told a guy that I'm really into." I can hear my voice getting shaky and louder. "He has said nothing back, cut off all contact with me with communication on social media. I don't understand why he still follows me, but he is."

"Why not just unfollow him yourself," she asks.

"I can't. I can't because I'm thinking maybe he will respond once he is ready and even if he isn't, he would just tell me himself to move on."

"You are what's holding you back from moving on. You're holding on to hope. The hope of something that may never go in your favor."

She is right. I won't lie. I'm hoping that Thomas will one day soon start communicating again. He wanted to meet with me at one time. She is also right about cutting off communication myself, but I can't. Why? I don't know.

"I met someone yesterday. I'm meeting him this afternoon for coffee."

"Tell me about him."

"There isn't much to tell, really, but his name is Jason. He is a white male and I have never dated outside of my race before."

I won't go in on my mother's or my friend's reactions right now. This session may be all day if I do.

"I'm not letting race stop me."

"So, you are going to continue to see or wait on the other guy, uh--. "

"Thomas, and yes, I really want to see where this goes with Jason but I'm not ready to stop trying with Thomas."

"You know, there are HIV treatments out there that helps patients become undetectable and once undetectable, it's harder to transfer the virus. Now, it's not a cure, but it's good to be undetectable so that transmission is less easy. That being said, you and the person still should practice safe sex," she says.

"I didn't know that."

"I know you're trying to keep the virus out of your mind, but it may be beneficial for you to learn more about it so that you understand it and once you understand, it may help you a little better with how you are feeling and educate those you reveal your status to."

She might be onto something. I guess knowledge is power. All I know is the virus is a death sentence and society has this stigma that it's a terrible thing and most positive people are like me, feel ashamed and because of our shame, we don't talk about it and keep it bottled up.

"Well, since Jason is fairly new, how about we talk about Thomas."

I don't want to tell her that Thomas is an actor. I know they say the sessions are between the therapist and the client, but I'm not ready to tell all of that. So, I fib a bit.

"I met Thomas downtown briefly, and I got his social media handle from a mutual friend," I say.

She nods, and I continue.

"I don't know him personally, but I just became attracted to him. I don't know why, and don't want to seem vain, but looks may have played a small part in it. When I see him online communicating with different people, he just seems so cool and down to earth. We chatted some, and he's cultured, funny, and I thought we were clicking. I didn't want to date him at first. I was fine with just communicating."

"Are you fine with just communicating because of your HIV status," she asks.

"Yes, I fell hard for him towards the end of this past summer, but I was willing to just accept the communication part of it without trying to pursue a relationship, but my heart is not letting me."

I tear up, but I don't stop talking. It feels good to get it all out there about how I really feel.

"He is an older man, and I've always been attracted to older men because some, not all, but some, seem like they treat their women better than the ones my age or younger."

"I see."

"I'm scared, though," I say, looking away from the screen again, "scared that I seem like that obsessed fan and I don't want to be that person. I feel I should stop trying with him, but I don't because he didn't tell me to stop, so I think maybe he wants me to still reach out and if he says to leave him alone, that is when I will stop because it's like confirmation for me and I will if he makes it clear to leave him alone."

I hate when I ramble, going on and on. I'm too old to be acting this way. Vonne, you are pathetic. Just leave that man alone. He isn't for you. Yeah, easier said than done.

"Do you think uninstalling the app would help," she asks.

"If I uninstall the app, I see myself reinstalling it maybe the next day or so," I say, returning eye contact.

"I think you should uninstall the app, see how Jason is at your first meeting and go from there," she says.

I know I won't be able to do it, but I nod, and I sit silent.

"I would like to stop here, Yvonne, and see you next Tuesday. What do you say?"

I honestly don't know if I want another session. This was hard for me, but I'm going to do it. I don't want to stop prematurely.

"Next Tuesday is fine, but can we continue with virtual sessions," I ask.

"Sure, if that's what you prefer.".

"Thanks, see you next Tuesday."

We disconnect, and I let out a deep, long sigh of relief that it's over. She might be right, though. Maybe I should just unfollow Thomas. He is acting differently anyway. I pull out my phone and open the 'MediaPal' messenger app and type my farewell message.

"Hi, Thomas. It has been a while since we've last communicated and after our last talk and your constant blowing me off with 'you're busy' messages, I have decided its time for me to stop trying and we both move on. It was nice and even though you have not said anything, I get the feeling that me leaving you alone is what you want. You won't get another message from me."

I stare at the send button for about a minute or two and I decide I can't send it and delete the message. I put my phone down on the desk. Why can't I just unfollow his ass and let that be it?

My phone rings, and it's Jason. I let it ring a few times before finally answering.

"Hello?"

"Hey, beautiful," he says cheerfully. "I know it's a bit earlier than what we set on, but is it possible I pick you up now?"

"Sure. Is it work?"

"Nah, I'm free today," he answers. "Just couldn't wait to see you."

I feel my cheeks expand as I can't help smiling. He seems sweet, but aren't they always in the beginning? I give my address and we hang up. I look to see if I need to retouch my makeup after that emotional session I had and stand on the porch to wait.

Moments later, Jason pulls up in a dark SUV. I'm making my way to the car when he jumps out and quickly makes his way to me.

"Is everything alright," I ask.

"Yeah, I just want to walk you to the car. I know a lot of women don't care these days, but I like to open the car door for them."

As I'm smiling, I look him over. He has an enormous smile himself. A smile so big that his eyes smile just as large. Chivalry isn't as dead as I thought.

"Not a problem at all. I welcome it."

Upon entering his car, I can get a huge whiff of a cherry scent. After putting my seatbelt on, I look up and see a red tree hanging from the rearview mirror. Car is clean. Not a crumb or spot anywhere. His house must be in order. Cash always said that you can tell how a person's house is by the way they keep their car.

***

We enter a nice quiet spot in Lincoln Park, an old brick building with immense picture windows. The inside has a very intimate setting. The walls are brick on the inside with abstract art displays on them. There are bright-colored seating of yellows, oranges, and reds. It's a tiny and cozy place and since I don't like crowded areas, this is perfect!

Jason sees me looking around. He leads us to an area in a corner near a large window where we sit on a soft love seat with a coffee table in front of us.

"I found this spot when I was looking for an apartment in the area," he says. "I would sit in here, have a cup of Joe, and look up apartments in the paper. Then I upgraded to the internet and started using a laptop."

We both laugh and he looks at me. I look at him. If I didn't meet him while he was making an arrest, I wouldn't have known that he was a cop. He's wearing a graphic tee and jeans with a buzz cut, tattoos, and a full beard. We could be around the same age. I might be a little younger.

"Do you have a favorite place to go to," he asks.

A young woman comes over to take our orders.

"Hi, can I have the cranberry muffin with latte," I ask.

She smiles and nods.

"And you, sir?"

"Just a coffee for me, black. Thanks."

"Coming shortly," the young woman says as she whisks away.

"Yes, a friend of mine owns her own coffee shop. It's further up north in the Rogers Park area. Her shop is bigger and busier, that's why I'm falling in love with this place. It's quiet and cozy."

We both sit and look at each other nervously until I decide to break the silence.

"How long have you been a in law enforcement?"

"It's been about twenty years. My dad was a cop, God rest his soul, and I have a twin who is also a detective."

"A twin?"

Please don't look alike. The last thing I need is to mistake one for the other.

"Yeah, my hair is darker, and I have more tats than he does. I hope to be doing what I do for a long time. My dad died on the job in his early 60s."

"I'm so sorry."

"Thanks. I really used to look up to him and I hope he sees that my brother and I are doing really well while following in his footsteps."

"I'm sure he is, and is very proud," I say with a smile.

The young woman is back in our little area with our order and sits our goodies down in front of us before rushing off.

"How old are you if you don't mind me asking," I ask.

"I'm 45," he answers. "I'll be 46 next year in January on the 2nd."

Ugh! Another Capricorn? My ex, my crush, and now Jason. I wasn't into the zodiac at first, but Karma is very much into it, and I remember the things she said about the Capricorn male: arrogant, selfish, aloof, and a bunch of others she has stated, and I have witnessed for myself.

I take a sip of my latte. I wish this place was in my neighborhood. It may make me want to leave the house because of the homey feeling.

"I'll be 38 in March," I say. "And I think this will be my new favorite place."

"I'm glad you like it," he says with a huge grin.

He sips his coffee and then looks over at me with uncertainty.

"Yvonne, it's been a while since I have sat down with a woman." he takes another sip of his coffee. "I mean, with a woman that I would like to get to know."

I look up from my latte. The sudden change in his tone worries me.

"I like to be upfront to keep from wasting each other's time. There is something that I need to say."

Great, this man is married. I bet he is. Why? It's like I'm not destined to be happy in this life. I want to just get up and leave, but not before thanking him for the latte. I do have some manners.

"Yvonne, I am HIV positive, and I have been for a very long time."

When he says this, I'm mid-sip of my latte before letting go of both cup and saucer. Hot latte all over me and it isn't bothering me at all. The crash of the dishes hitting the floor causes the few people who are inside to look over at us. My reaction, I'm sure, is saying "stunned" and I can't get a word out. Probably because my jaw is on the floor right next to the dishes. Another blood connection, only this one is not our blood that has connected, but our blood is both contaminated.

4

Unwelcome Back

I look at him and I'm sure my mouth is wide open. I've never had this happen to me before. It's usually the other way around, but now the roles are reversed. The young woman comes back to our area and collects the broken dishes casually.

"Miss, I'm so sorry about this," I say to our young server.

She nods but says nothing as she continues cleaning the mess I made. Jason has his head in his palm with the look of annoyance. What can I say? His words were so unexpected.

"Look if you want me to take you back home," he says while looking away from me.

I quickly sit up, "No, no!"

I place my hand over his, and he looks back my way with our eyes meeting again. I can feel his pain when he thinks I am ready to bolt after a statement like that, being through it many times.

"I'm not ready to leave," I say, smiling. "You just caught me off guard."

"I can see that. I'm just glad you're still here."

Of course, I'm not leaving. We are in the same boat. I don't know if what he told me should relieve me, make me happy, or what but even though there is a guy sitting next to me who is going through the same thing as I, I kind of wish it was Thomas sitting here. Well, here with me, minus the virus. I wouldn't wish this on anyone.

The server has finished cleaning the mess and walks away to continue other orders. Now that Jason and I are alone again, I decide that it's my turn to reveal something, too.

"I'm just like you, Jason, I'm also positive."

We both sit and say nothing. He looks at me with the look of uncertainty. Yes, I said I'm positive too. Now, are you going to leave? What is that look for?

"Really," he asks.

"Really," I answer.

"May I ask how you got infected," Jason asks.

I put a small piece of muffin in my mouth since it didn't hit the floor with my latte. "Well, I think it was the guy before my ex."

I take a bite this time of my muffin. Knowing it is a question that has to get asked doesn't make me ready to revisit that type of history.

"I'm not entirely sure, but he said something to make me believe he was the one to give me the virus."

"What was it he said?"

"He wanted to tell me something, but he couldn't get it out. After that, he had a real problem trying to have sex with me. It was weird. To this day, I still don't know what he was going to say."

"Wow," he says, then takes a sip of his coffee. "Do you want another latte?"

"No, I'm good, but thank you. How did you become infected?"

"My brother and I got it from birth. My father raped my mom. Not the one whom I mentioned earlier. He was my stepdad and treated us as if we were his own, but my father raped my mother and stalked her to keep from getting him put away. It's how she met my stepdad."

"Oh no! And he was okay with her being positive?"

"I guess so. He was with her until he died. Since his death, my mom has been alone."

My phone goes off and it's my doorbell, alerting me that someone is at my home. I excuse myself to see who it is. It's Karma and Cashmere. Wow, I knew they would come eventually to get me to change my mind about the fair. I don't bother answering the alert and turn my attention back to Jason.

"Everything okay," he asks.

"Yup, everything is fine. Just the mailman."

We stay and talk, spending the entire day with each other. He talks about family and his health, and I do the same. He ends up ordering me another latte, anyway. This is so unexpected. I haven't been on a date in ages. I only hope that good things come from this and lead us both into the future, together.

"Let me get you back. It was nice while it lasted. I need to get myself ready for tomorrow after I run some errands."

"Thanks for bringing me here, Jason. This is my new favorite place," I say with a smile.

Sorry, Rita.

He rises from his seat and extends a hand, which I then place mine onto his. He helps me on my feet after tipping the server, and we are off. I feel my stomach in knots from the meeting that just occurred. Could he be it? Am I wrong for still having Thomas in my head?

***

We arrive at my house, and I can see that Cashmere's car is still parked out front. I can't believe she is still here.

Jason parks, gets out, and walks over to my side. He opens the door to help me out. Such a gentleman. I smile and we head to my door. I look at Cashmere's car and there are two people inside. The other person has to be Karma.

"I really enjoyed myself today," I say to Jason,

"I hope we can do it again."

"I would like that."

We stand for a moment, not sure if we should kiss or not. I had a good time even if it was just coffee and conversation. I lean up to his cheek and give him a soft peck.

"I get a kiss, huh," he chuckles.

I can only imagine what my friends are saying in the car.

"Drive safe, Jason," I say, smiling.

"Good night, beautiful," he says as he heads downstairs.

I watch him until he drives away and not even a second later, car doors fly open, and my friends are frantically running to my door.

"Who was that," Cashmere asks loudly.

"Hi stalkers," I say, giggling. "I can't believe you all sat here until I got home. What if I went to his house?"

Cashmere laughs as she taps me on the shoulder. "You, go to someone else's house? You hardly even go out with us!"

They are both waiting for an explanation, with Cashmere having her hands on hips and Karma has her arms folded.

"Well, if you must know, he is a detective that I met at the store yesterday."

"You're dating white cops now," Cashmere asks with a stern look on her face. "They despise us"

"Not all," I mumble. "He is a good guy from what I can tell, even if he is a Capricorn."

"Capricorn," Karma exclaims. "Another one?"

"Like I know what a man's sign is before I talk to them," I say, laughing.

Cashmere looks around nervously. "Let's just get inside. I don't like the south side much. We can finish this discussion from behind the brick walls. I don't have a bulletproof vest in my wardrobe yet."

We all step inside and get comfortable in the living room. Cashmere helps herself in the kitchen and comes back with a tray of chips and dip.

"Love that you keep your kitchen stocked with goodies," Cashmere says with a mouth full of chips.

"Careful, your hips and ass are wide enough," I say while giggling.

"Ming is almost here. She should be here in five minutes," Karma says.

"When she gets here is when I'll talk about Jason," I say.

"Well, we will tell you why we came here today," Cashmere says, who is still stuffing her mouth with chips in between sentences.

"It must be urgent enough for you both to await my arrival," I say.

"Kia is back," says Karma, "and I had to pull Cash off her earlier."

Great! It's enough that I'm dealing with my health and love life. I don't want to deal with this whore of a bitch, too.

There were once five of us and we were all friends for a while, but Kia doesn't know... well, doesn't care that her friends' men are off-limits. She hurt Cash when she slept with her fiancé some years back, in the church's basement they were going to wed in. Needless to say, the marriage never happened. Oh, she got Karma too, except Karma's hubby wasn't having it. He told Karma right away. Kia was undressing and putting on a show while Karma was downstairs, talking to us in Ming's car. I guess some men are loyal.

After all of that and friendships fell apart, Kia left for New York. Now she is back and there ain't no telling what trouble she will cause this time.

The doorbell rings. I rush to the door to see who it is, completely forgetting that Ming is on her way.

"Let me get the door," I say.

I open the door, and it's Ming coming in with hugs and greets. We walk back to the other ladies, who also greet Ming. I want to know what brought Kia back. I don't think it's because she's changed, and she missed us. Why didn't her ass stay in New York?

"So why is Kia back," I ask.

"Oh, you know," Ming asks.

"Yeah, they made me aware when I got home today from an afternoon out," I say to Ming.

Ming grabs a chip from the tray that Cashmere prepared earlier and tosses it into her mouth.

"She lost her job, then her apartment, so she is back in Chicago to move in with her family temporarily until she gets back on her feet," Ming explains.

"Back home, huh," I say with a loud chortle.

What I forgot to mention is that when we were all around twenty-four, Kia had the audacity to sleep with her mom's then-boyfriend. The boyfriend tried to put her mom out of their house and keep Kia. So, I am wondering how all of this is going to play out because I know damn well her mom will not welcome her back with open arms. Fist, maybe, but not open arms.

"After what she did," Cashmere says, cackling. "A bitch about to be homeless."

We all fall out laughing. I better get ready to tell them about Jason, since Ming is here now. Also, how I am still feeling Thomas, because I know that they're going to ask about him and how he will affect my dating with Jason.

"Forget about Kia," I start, "I met someone, and he is so sweet."

"Aren't they always in the beginning," Ming asks.

"I really like him, and he is into me too."

"And he is a white cop," Cashmere says, interrupting me.

"Uh... can I finish?"

"Go on, Miss 'Jungle Fever'," says Cashmere.

"Wait, what about Thomas," Ming asks.

What did I tell you? I knew someone would ask.

"I still like him, too," I answer, "but I have not heard from him."

"If Thomas, we're to contact you tomorrow and ask you to go out, would you, even though you like Jason," Cashmere asks.

I fall silent. I know that if there's a slight chance in hell that Thomas reaches out to me, I will answer. Will I stop talking to Jason? No. We are not exclusive, and I won't just drop Jason because of a contact with Thomas. That's just crazy.

"And the answer, ladies and gentlemen, is yes... she would," Cashmere says, "Her silence says it all."

Karma burst out laughing. Then we all laugh.

"She is in love with two Capricorns now," Karma says.

"No, no," I say, "I just met Jason, but I am feeling him, though."

"Oh God, another one," Ming asks.

"Aren't you a Capricorn, Ming," Cashmere asks with raised eyebrows.

"Yeah, but male Capricorns are a handful," Ming answers.

I want to tell Ming the whole thing because she knows everything. I will have to sit and talk to her another time without the others.

"Well, watch your men, cause Kia's trifling ass is back," Cashmere says.

Well, Kia is black, so I don't think she would be Thomas' type, but Jason, she may try. But then again, men wouldn't turn down pussy, right?

"I don't plan on being around her, but the way I see it is if Thomas and Jason want to fuck her, who am I to stop it? If they want to be with just me, then I won't have anything to worry about."

"But why not stop it before it happens," Cashmere asks.

"Because, Cash, if I have to stop it one time, there will be other times that I'll have to stop and I'm not gonna be watching them 24/7 to protect my relationship. It will be exhausting, and they will find a way if they want it bad enough. Just don't see the point."

"What if it does happen," Karma asks. "What if Thomas or Jason do sleep with her?"

"Then I will just leave them be. This is why I stay single, even though I do want love. No one is loyal anymore. They go out here and fuck the first person they see over a stupid argument, or because they may find someone hotter. So, excuse me for feeling how I feel. I'm not going to stop anything. If they fuck, they fuck, and I'll just be done. I'm not chasing a man around."

This conversation is no doubt miserable, but I meant what I said. It leaves my friends with puzzling looks on their faces.

"I'm going to head home," says Cashmere, "but you better watch your guys."

"Thomas isn't even mine to worry about," I say. "He hasn't even sent a message in a long time now."

"Yeah, well, I know you still like him," Cashmere says, "but I'm going to get out of here. I need to drop Karma off."

"Okay, you two get home safe."

We hug and say our goodbyes. Now that it is just me and Ming, I can really get into what happened today.

"Girl, so let me tell you about Jason," I say as I jump onto the sofa.

"So, you are seeing this cop," says Ming, "but I know you have powerful feelings for Thomas."

"Who I have not met yet."

"He asked you out for coffee," says Ming.

"Yeah, until I told him about my HIV status. I am going to see where it goes with Jason because I feel like I'm an obsessed fan and it's obvious that Thomas isn't feeling me anymore."

Ming sighs and places her hand on my arm.

"I think you shouldn't give up on Thomas. He was messaging you things at first that seemed like he was into you at least as an actor and fan relationship, I'm not sure about flirtations, because I don't want to say something wrong, but just wait and see what he says while still getting to know Jason. Just to be sure."

I nod, but I'm pretty sure already.

"You have never dated a white man and with everything going on in the city with cop crimes against blacks, are you comfortable with him and trust him," Ming asks.

"I like him and I'm trying not to see color. We had a good coffee date staying the whole afternoon."

"It seems like you do like him."

"I do, and it turns out that we have something in common," I say.

I look down into my lap. I'm not happy Jason is positive, but it does ease some things.

"What's that," she asks while sipping on her soda.

"He is HIV positive, too."

Ming starts choking on her soda as she's trying to get a word out.

"Ming, are you okay," I ask her as I forcefully pat her back.

Once catching her breath, she sits closer to me.

"How did he tell you? How did he get it?"

"Well," I start, "he took me out for coffee, and he was feeling me. He said he wanted to tell me right then and there to get the truth out of the way."

"Oh my God," Ming exclaims. "Hell, if Thomas won't talk to you, at least you have someone who can relate."

"True, but I don't think I can be with someone that I haven't fallen for, and I am still feeling Thomas, strongly. And to answer your questions, he said that he got it from his mom when he was born with it."

"Wow," Ming says as she lowers her head. "I forgot that is one way you can catch it. Back in her day, I don't think there were ways to save the babies from the virus like they have now."

"He also has a twin who has it from birth."

Ming's eyes get huge.

"When do we all get to meet him," Ming asks. "Tell me about him. I mean, is he hot?"

I laugh while shaking my head and rolling my eyes.

"He is," I answer. "He's tall, which is a plus because I'm tall and it's hard to find men taller than me."

"What are you, like 5 foot 9 or 10 inches?"

"I'm 5 foot 9, and he looks to be about 6 foot 3 or 4, muscular build and body tatted like crazy, dark eyes and hair. Girl, he is sexy as hell and doesn't look like a cop at all when not in work attire. Looks more like a band member."

"Are you going to tell your mom," Ming asks.

"She knows, and she was not thrilled."

We sit snacking, and I want to know more about her guy. Here I am telling her about everything, and she has mentioned Jesse only once during the car ride home a few days back. I know she didn't like how open he was to everyone about his HIV status. Maybe she has decided it won't work out.

"So, what about you and Jesse," I ask while leaning over toward Ming with enthusiasm.

"Jesse and I are fine. We talked yesterday about how discreet I am with my status, and he says he only tells potential women and that, well in his words, 'I don't broadcast it for the world to hear', so I'm good with that."

"What does he do," I ask.

"Jesse works with a psychiatrist as a care coordinator. I think working in that office turned him to drugs. I've seen the place. Its patients are far gone. I wouldn't be able to work in a place like that."

"Yeah, I don't think I could either."

"Jesse is sweet, and I really like him now," says Ming as she tosses another chip in her mouth, "Even when he is the one who infected me. I probably could have been out dating if I wasn't so discreet."

"I never tried," I say as I grab a handful of chips out of the near empty bowl. "I feel no one would date me unless I was HIV negative."

"I think the reason you aren't having any luck, is because many people are ignorant when it comes to the virus. Did you know that there are drugs we are taking for the virus that keep us undetectable?"

"No," I answer, "I just thought they help us live longer. My therapist said the same thing. About being undetectable a good thing."

"Well, yeah, they do that too, but once you are undetectable, the virus doesn't show in your blood and makes it harder to transmit."

"I guess that makes me ignorant too," I say.

We both start cackling.

Ming rises to her feet. "I should get going."

"Yeah, I need to lie down," I say as I get up and stand beside her.

We walk to the front door when Ming turns to face me.

"Vonnie, don't wait too long on Thomas. If you want to wait, fine, but if Jason is treating you good, you should maybe give up on Thomas."

As I look away, I think, is giving up on Thomas what I want? If I'm not feeling Jason because of the love I want from Thomas, I should tell him. I don't want to be with him just because we are going through the same thing. It wouldn't be fair to him.

I look back towards Ming.

"I hear ya, Ming. It will work itself out."

We hug. She opens the door and walks out. I wait in the doorway until I see her in her car safe and watch as she drives away.

***

It's Friday evening, and I want to get out. I'm in a great mood since I've been seeing Jason for the past few days. We talked about our families and friends. We went for long walks along Lake Shore Drive, which is my favorite way to get to a certain spot where I like to think and talk to my grandmother. May she rest in peace. Nothing can stop this feeling I'm experiencing. Nothing!

Cashmere sees me and eyes me up and down when I walk up to the table at the coffee shop.

"What! What's got you out and about looking all good?"

"The first question should be, where did you just come from dressing all cute," Ming asks. "I love that outfit!"

I have the girls out today. What? It's a beautiful fall day, and I was out with Jason earlier and let me say that he didn't mind the girls being out one bit. The outfit I am wearing is simple for me. I think my friends just love the top, which is a purple and black lace silk corset-like. I added black lace arm warmers, black jeans, and ankle heel boots, also black. My dark curls are wild and free, and Jason loved every bit of it.

"Thanks, Ming," I say smiling. "I thought I would stop by here since I was out."

"We just got here ourselves," says Karma.

"I spent the day with Jason, and he needed to get home, so I came here."

I take my seat and order a hot chocolate. The girls are laughing and talking, and I'm in my own little world. I sigh as I look around. Conversations are fading as I'm thinking it's good to be back at our spot, all of us. Well, I was here before after being a shut-in for so long because of my depression, but back then something happened that almost separated us. Now here we are laughing and being happy. It's nice to be happy for once.

"Vonne, did you hear what I said," Cashmere asks.

I zap back out from my thoughts, clueless. "I'm sorry, Cash. What was it you said?"

"Have you heard or messaged, Thomas?"

"No," I answer, "I have not been on social media in a while."

Ming's eyes dart my way. "Really?"

"I'm serious, I have not."

I have been on social media looking at his posts because I've been thinking about him. I just don't feel like being judged, so yeah, I lied. Then I see someone coming up to our table through my peripheral view.

"Hey, ladies!"

I see Cashmere looking away from us and to the voice's direction while sniffing the air.

"What the hell is that stench? Smells like disease..."

We all look towards the voice and it's Kia.

"Oh, it's just Kia," Cashmere rolls her eyes as she finishes her statement.

"You all still come to this place, huh?"

We all fall silent when we see her. Smiles start fading and disgust slowly taking its place. I said nothing would ruin this day. This bitch just might.

"Hey Vonnie, you're looking well," Kia says with the biggest grin.

"Why are you here, Kia," I ask her, looking back at my hot chocolate.

I'm really not in the mood for her, and I can see that Cash is fuming. I want to keep it classy and cute, not be in an all-out brawl. Karma and Ming look Kia up and down as if she has some nerve.

"I can't stop over to say hi," Kia asks.

"No," Cashmere shouts, "You know good and damn well we don't like you and don't want to be around you!"

"Please take your trifling ass on," I demand.

"This is a public place," Kia says, still grinning.

"Then be trifling over there," Cashmere says while pointing to a table in a corner.

"Ladies, it has been years. Are you all still upset about all of that," Kia asks.

"Well, that depends. Is your mom still upset after what you did," I ask.

Rita is at a nearby table giving someone their order and starts snickering at my answer. She hurries back to the counter, trying to hold in her laughter. It seems that drama always happens to us in this place.

"My mother and I are just fine," Kia says.

"Oh? Well, word on the street is that the moment she saw you a few days ago, she snatched you up, and it took 3 men to get her up off your ass," Cashmere says with a huge grin that matches Kia's.

Kia's grin is going away now. The nerve of this chick. She does all these things to people that were close to her and expects us to forget it and move on. Acting like nothing ever happened, or like it was no big deal at all. She is a whore, and I don't trust her. I still meant what I said when we were all at my house. I will not be watching Jason or Kia. If he wants me, then he should be able to block temptation. Now, that doesn't mean that I want her around.

"I wanted to see if anyone had a spare room until I got back on my feet here, but it seems that won't be an option for me," Kia says with an inaudible sigh.

"You've got that right," Cashmere mumbles.

Karma, who is sipping on her tea, spits it out while laughing in disbelief.

"Are you out of your fucking mind," Ming asks, "You must be if you think we are going to offer a room to you after the shit you've done."

"I thought you were going to your mom's to stay," Karma asks.

"I guess you and her aren't okay, like you say," Ming adds.

"Now, Kia," Cashmere starts, "you know all you have to do is open your legs and some guy will let you stay with them for free."

I let out a cackle that I can't control. Seriously, I didn't mean to laugh at that comment, it just came out.

"Kia, just go away. It doesn't have to be out of here, just out of our faces. Please and thank you," I say nonchalantly as I wave my hand towards a nearby table in an attempt to shoo her away.

"Fine, I need to figure out my arrangements anyway," Kia says. "I guess I'll see you at the Lover Fair, or whatever it is."

She gives us all one last look before turning and heads for the door.

"Unbelievable," Cashmere says shaking her head. "It's as if she did nothing wrong."

"Yeah, and now we have to see her ass at the damn fair," Karma asks.

This would mean that I may have to show my ass at the fair and I don't wanna to do that with Jason there with me, but if I must beat her ass, it would be good that he is there.

"If she is there, we will just ignore her," says Ming.

"All of us this year? Together? I love it," Karma says while imitating Kia's grin.

I notice what Karma is trying to do and laugh. "I see you Karma. Please don't do that."

"That grin looks so evil on her face," says Karma.

"Fitting for an evil bitch," Ming mutters as she's looking at her phone

"Was looking forward to it, but I don't know now," I say.

"Fuck her," Cashmere shouts, "we can, and will, ignore the trick. She might not even show anyway now that she sees that her friends and her own damn family hate her."

"I know I said to myself that no one will get me down today, but I think Kia has succeeded," I say, sipping my hot chocolate.

We all had the look of solemn. That dark cloud has taken our sunshine away. The mood of the group changed. Then Ming stands up, looking at the rest of us.

"Why are we so down now? We will not let some borderline hooker ruin our day."

Cashmere scoffs at Ming's remark. "No need to be subtle, Ming. Borderline, my ass. She is a full-blown whore!"

We all just sit quietly. Cashmere is shaking her head. I'm guessing she's still upset her about what just transpired or what happened with her ex-fiancé.

"Come on ladies," Ming exclaims as she sits back down, "don't think about her. Gosh, we need a bar."

I decide to change the subject because Ming is right. So, I talk about what I will wear to the Couple's Fair.

"Ming, I know you bought me an outfit for the fair tomorrow, but I decided I'm going to wear something else," I say.

"You're fine and I understand," Ming says, grinning. "I'm guessing you are going to dress a little sexier now that you have a date?"

"Ding, ding, ding," I say, giggling. "The maxi skirt is cute, but if the weather permits, I'll be showing my legs."

"I don't know what I'll be wearing, yet," says Karma, "but whatever it is, it will be a fall outfit. Mostly browns, reds, and tans."

"Yes, ladies, we are coming to slay," says Cashmere while high-fiving me and Karma.

I look at the time and see it's getting late. I collect my things. We are back on track, and everyone is smiling again, but I need to leave since I'm the only one without a car and buses in this area don't run late.

"Are you leaving, Vonne," Ming asks.

"Yes, it's getting late, and I need to get some rest so I can enjoy myself tomorrow."

"We should all meet up by the entrance at about 8 pm," says Cashmere, "because I want to meet Jesse and Jason."

I give everyone hugs and wave to Rita while she is collecting our dishes before walking out.

As I am walking to the bus stop, I hear a familiar giggle. I turn to look and it's Kia, flirting with a guy sitting on the hood of his car. He is accepting the flirts but not as "handsy" as she is. I roll my eyes, wondering whose man is she messing with now. When the man raises his head to look around, I can't believe who it is. It's Jason, the detective that I am dating. He doesn't see me, but I sure as hell can see him. Fuming, I walk on to the bus stop and wait. I just need to get out of this area.

5

Emotional Closure

"They are out there right now," Ming asks.

"Yes, a building down from the coffee shop," I snap.

"What the fuck," Cashmere yells. "I'm going out there right now!"

I'm on the bus whimpering, but it's already too late. The few people that are on the bus with me can hear how upset I am. I can't wait to get home to tell them. I am so pissed off, not even knowing if it's as bad as I think it is.

"Cash, wait," Ming shouts, "we should go out calmly!"

"No, don't bother! Going to call him now myself. Please don't do anything. Just stay in the shop."

Jason is a detective, after all. I don't need my friends in jail for assault. Besides, I want to hear from his own mouth what is going on.

"Okay, girl. I got Cash blocked in. Let us know what is happening."

I'm wiping tears and trying to calm down. This isn't bad. I didn't see him all over her like she was him, but he didn't stop her, either.

"Vonnie, are you there," Ming asks

"Yeah, okay," I say, "I'm hanging up now."

"Call or text me when you get home."

"Me too," Cash yells into the phone, even though it's on speaker.

I hang up, but decide to wait until I get home to talk to Jason. Too many people are already looking at me and I want no more of my business out on this bus. Two more transfers before I'm home to even call Jason. This is going to be a long ride.

***

I wake up to about a dozen texts and an equal amount of missed calls. Last night I didn't call anyone and I'm guessing the missed calls and texts are because no one has heard from me since the conversation during my bus ride. I didn't even call Jason, but I will right now.

I honestly can't be mad at Kia. I never introduced her to Jason. It's not like she knows that he and I are dating. But Jason knows, so why would entertain her like that?

"Hello?"

"Good morning, Jason. How are you?"

"Hey Beautiful! I'm good now that I hear your sexy voice. Are we still going to that couple's thing tonight," Jason asks chuckling.

"Well, that depends on a few things."

"Is everything okay," he asks.

"I saw you outside last night, sitting on your car hood with a woman all over you in Rogers Park on Lunt Ave near Ridge BLVD, and don't try to say it was your twin brother because I know it was you."

There is a brief silence on his end. Probably trying to think of something that will calm me down.

"Vonne, why didn't you just come over to me," Jason asks.

"Why was she all over you," I ask, completely ignoring his question.

"She was just talking with me and then she started flirting and touching me --. "

"But you did nothing!"

Silence again. I don't want to be that chick that can't trust a guy. That is a sure way of ending a relationship, but if he is with me, why not move away? Maybe I'm thinking our relationship is one way, and he thinks it's another. Are we exclusive or just trying each other out?

"Jason, what are we doing," I ask calmly. "I know we have known each other a very short time, so I may be out-of-pocket here. Are we trying each other out, but having our options open?"

"Well, we are still getting to know one another, but nothing was going on between me and that woman. I'm trying to get to know you and I really like you. You have nothing to worry about."

He still didn't tell me why he allowed Kia to be on him like that, but we aren't exclusive anyway, so I have no right, I guess.

I can hear Jason clearing his throat. "Listen, next time you see me, just come over. I'm always happy when I see you. Now get ready so we can see each other tonight."

"Okay," I say, "see you tonight."

I've been hurt and I do have a slight self-esteem issue. I think I'm in the wrong here. If I don't stop, the relationship will end before it starts.

"Hey, what happened to you," Ming asks. "I have been calling and texting you since last night."

"Well, you got me on the phone now," I say with a bit of irritation.

"Just tell me what the hell happened," Ming demands. "Did you call him? What the hell did he say?"

I put the phone on speaker so that I can lay out the clothes I'm wearing tonight.

"Everything is fine," I say. "Kia doesn't know that I'm seeing him, so it's not like she did anything malicious. But I will say I didn't like that Jason didn't stop what she was doing to him."

"I don't like that either, but you all did just start seeing each other. It still makes me think he may not want an actual relationship. I would keep my eyes on him if I were you, Vonne. Hell, I'll be watching his ass, too!"

"You do that," I say with a low chuckle. "In the meantime, I'm hanging up now so I can get ready."

"Bye, girl," Ming says before disconnecting.

I hang up and sit on the bed. How can I get mad at Jason since I'm about to do something myself? I look through 'MediaPal' to see what Thomas is up to. He hasn't really posted much, just liking a lot of Hollywood stuff. I send him a message. I hate this silent mess. Say something, damn it!

"Hi, Thomas! I hope you are well. I would like to talk because I just can't leave what I told you alone without a response of some kind."

Why am I even trying? I look at my account at all the silly posts I've created. That was when I was in a good mood and me and Thomas were getting along. Now my page is full of sad thoughts, depression notes and memes.

"They say to go after the one you want, but it's hard when the person is just not interested. Persistence does not always pay off." I post on my 'MediaPal' page.

As I'm putting my phone down, I hear it chime. No, it's not Thomas, just a few people liking my post. I sit the phone back down and head for the shower.

***

"I'm outside," says Jason on the other end of the call.

"Will be out in a sec," I say.

I give myself one last look in the mirror. Oh, I'm turning heads tonight! I have both legs out in a long brown maxi skirt with thigh-high splits on both sides and a skin-tight, low cleavage top under a knit sweater jacket that stops right under the girls.

I open the door to step out, and there's Jason, wearing jeans and a sweater. He always looks good. We both smile at one another, except I'm blushing.

"Wow, you look great," says Jason.

"Thank you and so do you."

I slip my hand into his, and we both make our way down the stairs to his car.

***

When we arrive, I see Cash and one of her dates at the entrance. After what happened in the church on her wedding day between her fiancé and Kia, Cash decided not to be in a committed relationship. She calls her men lovers. This lover that is on her arm tonight is one I have not met. Cash sees us and runs our way while screaming with excitement.

"Finally, you are here with the group," says Cashmere while pulling me into a tight hug

"What is she talking about," Jason asks.

"Well, I was a shut-in," I explain. "I used to never go out with the girls because of my discomfort with crowds and terrible anxiety, with panic attacks."

"Oh?"

"Yeah. I was on medications, but I didn't like the side effects, so I stopped taking them. My doctor wants me to speak with a psychiatrist to get new meds, but I refuse and that's a whole other story."

"I don't know where Ming and Karma are," says Cashmere, "but they need to hurry their asses up."

I stray off, looking around. The setup looks like a carnival inside an enormous building, except it's dressed up in a lot of hearts and balloons. You can sit outside or take pictures. There are tents with adult toys to browse and buy, and not too far from that is a lingerie tent. There are games and food. So much to see and do. We have to get past the security booth where they check our ID because the fair is pretty much for adults.

"Hey, remember me?"

I turn back to the group, and I see Kia in Jason's face again and Cashmere marching towards Kia with clenched fists. I quickly join Jason's side again. Has Cash forgotten he's a cop?

"Everything okay over here," I ask as I'm giving Kia the evil eye.

Kia groans. "Do you two know each other?"

I smile while looking up at Jason. "Yes, we do, and he is my date tonight."

At first, Kia just stands there eyeing the both of us. Then she finally says with a shrug, "Well, he doesn't have a ring on his finger."

Cashmere laughs. "Somehow I don't think that would matter."

"That is old news," Kia says.

"And you are still the same bitch that can't keep her hands to herself," Cashmere snaps. "Now back off!"

Jason whispers in my ear, "Vonne, do you know her?"

"Yes, I do, and she is not well-liked."

I don't want to go in on Kia's entire background with Jason here at the fair. I just want to enjoy myself. Thankfully, I see Ming and Karma walking up with their date and husband.

"Everyone is looking good," says Ming as she walks up to the group with a massive smile, hand in hand with Jesse.

"Let me introduce everyone," I start. "Jason, these are my closest friends Ming, Cash, and Karma. The stray is Kia."

There are a few low snickers. Kia rolls her eyes and goes to the booth to be let inside.

"I'll let everyone introduce their dates," I say.

"Nice to meet you, ladies," Jason says while shaking hands.

"This wonderful guy who is accompanying me is Jesse," Ming says with a smile.

"Hey, man. How's it going," Jesse asks while extending his hand.

"Good, Good," Jason replies.

"I'm Terrell, I'm here with Karma."

"And I'm Troy, here with the lovely Cash."

"Oh, stop," Cashmere says with a chuckle.

"Ya'll ready to head inside," Ming asks.

"Lead the way," Jason answers.

We all walk to the booth and show our identifications. When we finally make it inside, you can smell food, hear whips snapping, and see a lot of couples openly showing some affection that I think should be for the bedroom.

"Wow," I shout.

The place looks exciting, and I'm glad that I can be here. I'm also glad that I'm not here dateless.

"See what you've been missing, Vonne," Cashmere asks.

A woman in a leather corset with a thong is clearing her throat at the microphone on a stage that is dressed in red and black lace.

"Welcome to this year's 'Couple's Fair' and do we have a treat for you!"

The crowd cheer and applauds. She shushes everyone by putting a red glitter scepter to her bright red lips.

"This year we have a burlesque group who will perform for you, but that's not all. We will also be open for two weeks instead of one to give everyone a chance, who is of age, to visit the fair. For more info, there is a board with flyers. Thank you for coming and enjoy. Now get those sexy asses out there and explore!"

There's a low rumble throughout the building thanks to the visitor's reactions and applause. The crowd disperses from around the stage and bustle to the nearby stands of naughty goodies the fair has to offer.

"How long are you guys staying," I ask everyone.

"Are you kidding? Troy and I will be here all night," says Cashmere with a laugh. She then pulls Troy by his shirt toward the tent with the adult toys.

We all shake our heads and laugh.

"We will be here for a while," says Karma.

Cashmere and Troy are making their way back with trays.

"Penis dogs!!!! And for the men, the pussy sandwich!!!"

I couldn't help but laugh. The ladies and I decide to take a picture of us holding the penis dogs.

"Troy, here, take our picture," Cashmere demands.

The polishes are huge, and they made one end look exactly like the tip of a penis while the other end is the scrotum on a stick. They are creative with the sandwiches, too. The meat is folded and shaped like a vagina inside a shaped bread full of poppy seeds to mimic vaginal hairs, and white sauce, which is mayo, oozing out of the center.

We all do funny poses with the dogs except Karma, who is clearly embarrassed and just holds her penis dog with her hand over her face.

"I am going to post mine on my page," I say while laughing.

"You know I did already," says Cashmere after taking a huge bite.

The guys are having fun mimicking sex-play with the pussy sandwiches and are making our group and nearby patrons laugh.

"I can't breathe," says Ming, while laughing and gasping for air.

Cashmere and Troy are having a little fun of their own, with Cashmere sticking her penis dog into Troy's pussy sandwich.

"Cash!!!! I swear we can't take you out in public," Karma says while blushing and shaking her head with embarrassment.

"What," Cashmere asks.

Karma grabs Terrell's hand and they both dart past the group's show, with Terrell stumbling behind her.

"What a prude," Cashmere says after taking another bite of her penis dog.

"You thirsty," Jason asks me as he devours the last of his sandwich.

"I'll just have a bottled water," I say right before receiving a soft peck from his soft lips.

Jason hurries away, trying to get in the already long line before more people share his idea. I see Kia not too far from the concession stand with a bright pink short halter dress on, black fishnet stockings and pink heels. Some men in her vicinity are falling over themselves, looking at her almost perfectly round behind as she walks by them.

There are so many people here that my anxiety is creeping up now and I realize I'm standing alone while I wait for my water. Ming and Jesse are throwing darts for adult toys and Cashmere is giving Troy and other men who notice her on a pole, a show. I don't see Karma or Terrell anywhere.

I walk around, seeing all that I can see while I wait for Jason, who is still in line. I decide I want to sit down, so I go to a nearby bench and that is when I see Thomas Edgar with a woman on his arm. He isn't in any kind of disguise like I picture most actors and actresses. He's wearing a cap, a black top and jeans. No one seems to notice him. The woman who is with him I've never seen, which makes me believe she isn't an actress or anything, just his date.

I stand there and look at them both, contemplating if I should walk over there to him or not. Most people would tell me he doesn't want to be bothered since he stopped communicating, but we were chatting, and he stopped right after I told him I'm HIV positive and I had a few things I wanted to get off my chest. So... I go over to him.

I'm closing in on Thomas and his date. His date is smiling at him, not even noticing me heading straight for them. Thomas, however, sees me, and his entire demeanor changes.

"Hi, Thomas. We need to talk."

Both are looking at me. Thomas' look is more like glaring. I turn to his date and introduce myself.

"Hi, I'm Yvonne. Please don't be alarmed. I just need a minute with Thomas, then you can be back on his arm again," I say, while forcing a smile.

"I'm sorry, Renee, I'll only be a moment," Thomas says before turning towards me with a sour look on his face.

Thomas and I both walk to a small space in a corner away from the crowd, but still in view of Renee. She looks our way before focusing on me. Renee's eyes meet with mine, then she quickly turns away.

"So, what is it, Vonne," Thomas demands.

"I'm sorry to irritate you, but you just stopped all contact after I told you about my health."

"And you just thought you'd make me talk to you," Thomas asks.

"Look, Thomas, I'm not angry because you may not want to get to know me romantically anymore because I know many people who wouldn't date someone like me."

He turns to look at Renee, then back to me. Renee is sitting with her hands on her lap, patting her thighs as if she is growing impatient.

"Then why are you upset," Thomas asks.

"I'm upset because instead of you talking to me and telling me how you feel about what I told you, you just completely shut down!"

"Can we do this later," Thomas asks.

No! We need to do this now!

He starts to walk away, but I grab his arm. He turns and faces me with an irritated look, then his expression softens.

"Vonne, I will message you about this later," he says. "I mean it."

We look at each other. I can't read him or what he may be thinking. We just stand there until finally; I release his arm.

"Okay, Thomas," I say, softly.

Thomas gives me one last look before heading over back to Renee, leaving me where I stand. I watch them for a moment. They both look at me before walking away.

I head back over to where the concession stand is, but no Jason. After looking in the area for him, I see him and Kia chatting it up in a corner of their own, looking a little too cozy.

"Sorry to interrupt," I say dryly.

They both turn to look at me. Kia is rolling her eyes, upset at the interruption.

"Well, you seemed to be preoccupied with the guy you were talking to, so Kia thought she would keep me company until you were done," Jason says with irritation.

I'm already not in a great mood and I don't feel like going at it with him or Kia. So, I walk away, not saying another word.

"Vonne! Vonne!" Jason shouts, knocking over Kia as he is trying to follow me.

I continue walking while ignoring Jason. Now, I just want to go home. I'm feeling like everything is falling apart. Reaching into my purse, I pull out my phone to get an Uber home. My friends are all having a good time and I don't want to ruin it for them. Thomas and Renee look to be in a serious conversation. I hope I didn't mess anything up between the two of them. Then I see Jason looking for me in the crowd. I hurry outside so I can wait on my ride to leave quietly.

***

My phone is ringing nonstop. Instead of enjoying my Sunday in a quiet house and relaxing, my friends and Jason keep calling. My mom called earlier this morning to check on me and to talk about her time she's spending with my aunt. Also, no message from Thomas.

I have a therapy session coming on Tuesday and I'm not sure if I'm ready to deal with that again. I haven't done my homework, which is to cut Thomas off completely. He was angry that I forced him into a conversation I've been wanting to have with him and if he would've just answered my messages, last night probably would have ended differently. He had a date with him, Renee. It relieved me to see that she's a "sista" since most women he follows on 'MediaPal' are white women who like to be half-naked on their pages.

Then there is the Jason and Kia thing. I don't even know what I want to do about me and Jason, but as of right now, I have nothing to say to him. Thomas and I were talking. That was it. We were not in a corner all close and cozy. I think part of the reason I'm not answering my friend's calls is that I will have to tell them why I left, and it may cause court cases and jail sentences when they know Kia is involved.

I hear my doorbell and I just know it's Jason or my friends. I try to peek out the window to not be seen, and it's Thomas! How the hell does he know where I live?!

I open the door and we just stand looking at each other. He is a very handsome man. I love his eyes and the way he is looking at me, even if he is pissed, and his full lips that I could just--.

"Are we going to stand here all day or are you going to invite me in," Thomas asks.

I say nothing as I back up, opening the door wider so that he can walk in.

"Have a seat," I say.

Thomas walks over and chooses the center seat of the sofa. I sit in the matching chair and turn to face him. He's clearly still upset from last night. He won't look at me at this moment. We sit quietly, then I decide to speak.

"How did you find me?"

"I followed the car you left in last night. When you made it to your house, l sat and watched you go in. I was going to ring the bell, but I waited until today."

"Thomas, why didn't you just chat with me? I miss your messages. I miss how we would joke around and how you would tell me about your day and your projects..."

"Listen, you are a beautiful, sweet young woman that I really liked. Hell, I still do. When you told me you were HIV positive, I just... I don't know. I guess I didn't know what to say about it."

We both sit quietly. Then I hear car doors closing. I stand up instantly, and I can hear Cashmere talking with Ming.

"Come with me, quickly," I whisper.

I grab his arm as he rises out of his seat. We run upstairs, where I know no one can see us through any windows. I finally have Thomas here and he is talking. I will not fuck this up!

We sit in my room while my friends constantly ring the bell. Thomas sits in my furry pink chair that's shaped like a gigantic stiletto heel, and I sit on my bed.

I look down into my lap. "I just don't feel like company from them right now." When I finally decide to look up, I see Thomas staring at me. He looks at me as if I'm something foreign, or like he's studying me. I feel so awkward, but I sit quietly and look away.

After about 10 minutes of the awkward silence and the constant doorbell ringing, I hear car doors slamming shut again. I sigh and look back at Thomas, who still has his eyes on me.

"Listen, I'm sorry," Thomas starts. "I have been busy working with a lot of different projects and doing other things when I have time for myself. I don't want you to stop messaging me and I could have sent a message. You caught me off guard and I didn't know what to say."

I understand him completely. I'm not mad that he can't be with me. I'm upset because he cut me off. It made me really hate myself. Well, when guys act that way, it makes me hate myself. Yes, I've fallen for him. I can't make my heart change its mind, no matter how I try. He could have just been there, you know. Yeah, he is not obligated to be, but I would have felt better than how I'm feeling now.

"I know. Been through this before. I've already started thinking I won't have love in this life."

"What about the guy that you were with at the fair," Thomas asks.

"He seems to be into an ex-friend. Don't think there is anything between us."

"And he accepts you," Thomas asks. "Did you tell him about your medical issue?"

"Yes, he knows."

I didn't tell Thomas that Jason is also positive because that's not for me to do.

"Have you dated anyone that is HIV negative?"

I sigh. I sigh because I have back when I was in denial. Back when I was in my twenties, I dated a guy. We met at his job at a supermarket. I found out later that he was into drugs and was with multiple women, so I let him go.

"I have," I answer, "but it didn't work out because his interest didn't stop with me."

"I see."

We both sit in my room quietly. I can tell that Thomas is deep in his thoughts. The time now is 3:00 pm. I have eaten nothing yet, but I'm not hungry because I'm sitting in my bedroom with Thomas freaking Edgar! Though I thought meeting him would be more exciting than this. The meetings with him have been full of embarrassment for me.

Thomas clears his throat and lays back in the chair with crossed arms behind his head. "Hey, what do you have to drink?"

As I look at him, I know I sure as hell don't have a juice bar or fancy water with fruit and veggies floating in it. I'll just give him a bottled water. Can't go wrong with that, right?

"I have bottled water," I say to him as I rise from my bed.

"I'll take that, thanks."

I run downstairs to get a couple of bottles of water. I look out the window in the living room and I see Jason's car outside, but no Jason. What is he doing here, and where the hell is he? No matter, I'm not opening the door for his ass, anyway. I walk into the kitchen to look out the window there. Maybe he's in the back, although I don't know why he would be back there. Nothing. No one is in the yard. I shrug and grab a couple of bottled waters out of the fridge and rush back upstairs. When I walk in, I see Thomas looking around my bedroom.

"Here's your water," I say as I walk up to hand him his bottle.

Thomas turns to face me. He walks up to within range of the water that's waiting for him to retrieve. As he reaches out to take the bottle, he grabs my hand instead and pulls me close. He's looking into my eyes that has widen in disbelief. What the hell is happening?

6

Decisions

We are looking each other in the eye. I'm wondering if this is a pity moment. Is he pitying me because of what I've been through, or does he feel guilty because of how he treated me? I don't want pity love. He had an issue when I disclosed my status to him, so why am I in his arms now?

"Wait, what are you doing," I ask as I'm pulling away from him.

He pulls me back in, but instead of pulling me by the arm as he did before, he has his arms around my waist.

"Let me just hold you for a minute."

"Huh? Why? You didn't want to communicate before, and now you want me in your arms? What about Renee?"

"Renee is just a friend who wanted to check out the fair and didn't want to go alone."

Bullshit! I know he's lying, and I don't want to pull back again, but I'm not comfortable in this position either. I won't lie, it feels good; him holding me. I clear my throat as I move back from him. This time I won't let him get me again.

"So, um, here's your water," I say, sitting it down on my desk after breaking totally free.

"Are you okay, Vonne," Thomas asks.

"No! You didn't seem to want anything to do with me, and yes, I know what you already told me about why you did it, but now here you are with your arms all over me. What the hell, Thomas?!"

"I told you I'm feeling you," Thomas replies. "Just because you tell me you are HIV positive doesn't mean that I'm not still interested in you. I just don't really know how to go about it, but I still want to hold you. Is that alright with you?"

I let out a huge, exasperated sigh. I'm looking at Thomas, looking at me, and I just don't know what to say. Then there is another issue that he doesn't know about, and that Jason is lurking somewhere outside my house.

"I did a little research on the virus, and it was interesting," Thomas continues walking back up on me again, "but am I ready and willing to put myself in that situation?"

"You like me? Fine, but don't do something you think you are not ready for or will regret later."

"Look, we will revisit this later. Right now, I have a few interviews I need to do tomorrow via video, and I want to get home and relax."

He backs away from me slowly, still looking at me. He then turns around and walks towards my bedroom door to exit before grabbing his bottled water off my desk. He turns back to me again, with a smile this time.

"It's nice to finally meet you, Miss Vonnie."

"Same," I mumble.

I'm pretty sure the look on my face is confusion because then Thomas walks up to me, puts the bottled water in his pants pocket and grabs my hands.

"It will be alright. Don't stop messaging me. I promise to respond when I can."

He lets go except for one hand, which he uses to lead me downstairs. We are at the front door now and I'm dreading opening it. I know Jason is out there, but what the hell is he doing? Thomas opens the door to let himself out. He turns and gives me a slight nod with a smile, then walks to his car. I watch him from my doorway until he leaves, then suddenly I'm being rushed into the house! It's Jason, seething!

"I come here because I'm feeling guilty about how things happened last night, and your ass is here with the man from the fair," Jason asks in outrage.

"You and Kia were in the corner talking. Why are you guilty of that? Why are you guilty of talking?"

Jason paces back and forth. He is so livid that it's scaring me.

"Kia... she was with me last night," Jason says. "I was upset because I couldn't find you and she needed a ride home--."

"Stop," I yell, fighting back tears. "I knew you were too good to be true!"

"Wait, Vonne--."

"NO! I don't want to hear it," I scream.

I storm to the door and open it, standing in silence, waiting for him to leave.

"Vonne, just wait," Jason pleads.

"No, please just go!"

We stand and look at each other, then I turn away. I just want him gone. I'm not kicking him out because I'm going to go run to Thomas. I am seriously upset that he couldn't control himself while with that bitch and made it seem like I was jealous and having trust issues.

Jason walks to the door, takes one last look at me, then leaves. I shut the door behind him. I don't know what I'm going to do now. My life, believe it or not, was a hell of a lot less stressful when I didn't have men in it.

***

It's around 7:00 pm and I need to get my mind off everything. I sit with my blanket and cellphone on the sofa thinking about all that happened last night and earlier today. I don't know what to think about Thomas. He was being weird today. I should be excited, right? Thomas was here in my home, my crush... I just don't know what to expect, really. I don't think I'll message him for a while. If he really wants to try us, then I want it to be because he wants to, not because I'm constantly pestering him.

I'm liking Jason too. He was there when Thomas wasn't communicating with me, but he's easy with temptations. I don't like that. Wonder if he told Kia that, he's positive.

As I'm laying on my sofa, there is a knock on the door. I need to charge that damn bell again. I hate it when I can't screen visitors.

"Why haven't you answered our calls and texts," Ming shouts as she's storming into my house.

"I didn't feel like talking about it."

"We didn't know that you even left last night."

"Yeah, well, Jason pissed me off, and I just needed to get out of there. I didn't tell you guys because I didn't want to spoil it for the rest of you."

"So, what the hell happened?"

"Girl, I saw Thomas at the fair last night."

"What, no way!"

"Yes, and he was there with a woman."

"So that's why he wasn't messaging you back. He could've just told you he had his eyes on someone else instead of ignoring you!"

"I guess, but let him tell it she just wanted company."

"Did you get to talk to him about what you two chatted about," Ming asks.

I let out a deep sigh.

"More than talk. We held each other. Not at the fair. He was pissed there, but then he came over here. I don't know, it was a surprise to me how he just wanted to hold me and talk."

"Wait, the man ignores you all this time and when you meet, he is all interested now," Ming asks.

Ming sits there, shaking her head in disbelief.

"And Jason saw Thomas leave out," I add.

"What the hell," Ming says as she cackling, "But I thought you liked Jason? You both are going through the same thing."

"I did — I mean... I do, but he fucked Kia!"

Ming jumps out of her seat, nearly standing at attention. I can see her turning red. She is fuming.

"What?! That--," Ming starts before getting cut off.

"That's why I left last night. When Jason was in line getting our water, I saw Thomas, and I thought it was the perfect opportunity to see what was going on."

"Then what," Ming asks while attentively sitting back down in her seat.

"Then Jason saw us, and I guess he was trying to make me angry because he and Kia were cozying up in a corner, and it worked. I left without no one seeing me, so I thought, but it turned out that Thomas did and followed me here."

"Wow, Vonne, I gotta say, this is the most drama that you've had in a long time," Ming says while chuckling. "Who are you going to choose?"

"No one. Thomas says he researched HIV, and he learned what I just learned from my therapist and you. That it is possible to date if I stay undetectable, but he doesn't seem like he will take the risk. I don't blame him either."

My phone chimes and I see a message from Thomas. I ignore it for now.

"And then you have Jason that seems to not be able to control himself when a woman touches him. He isn't good at resisting temptation," I add.

"Wow, just wow," Ming says.

"Yeah, it sucks. Makes me scared to be in a relationship, because I don't want to get hurt again."

I look at my message. *"Hi, Vonne. I haven't forgotten you. I'm still thinking about this. Message me anytime. Bye for now."*

I just stare at my phone.

"What is it," Ming asks.

"It's Thomas. What if he tries it with me?"

"Okay, what did that message say?"

"Nothing, I'm going to wait until he reaches out to me about it."

It's funny how I was constantly messaging him and wanted him to communicate, but now I'm good. If he is truly thinking about it, I don't want any influence from me. I need to give him space so he can think it out on what he wants to do and be sure about it.

Ming rises from her seat. "It's getting late. Monday is usually my busy day, so I need to head home and relax before work tomorrow."

"Okay, girl," I say while walking her to the door, "Drive safe and call or text when you get home."

***

It's after 11 pm. Ming is home safe, Jason has been texting me nonstop, and Cashmere and Karma, I'm pretty sure, are pissed because I didn't open the door earlier.

I haven't eaten the entire day. I'm wondering what is going on in Thomas' mind. I go through my social media, but he hasn't posted since Friday, and I see Kia has followed Jason on 'MediaPal' but Jason isn't following Kia. I think I'm about done with everything. Too wired to sleep with so much on my mind, but I get into bed, anyway.

***

I haven't been in the mood to hang out with friends and I'm not sure if I'm in the mood for this therapy session either. It's a Tuesday morning, and it's pouring outside. This dreary day is matching my mood perfectly.

I decide I will see Bethany. Maybe she will have some advice about my dilemma, but I'm keeping on my pajamas. I just don't give a fuck today.

I log into my account and wait for my session to begin. It's only a two-minute wait before I see Bethany on the screen.

"Good morning, Yvonne! How are you?"

"Hi, Bethany, I'm okay I guess."

I'm already regretting logging in, but I can't help but wonder what this session is going to be like.

"Aw, it sounds like you're having a bad day. How about we start with what is bothering you," Bethany suggests while grabbing a notepad and pen.

"Well, I failed my homework."

"Hm, I believe you were to unfollow a man you have been communicating with online and uninstalling the social media apps."

"Yeah, but it's not from lack of trying."

"But you didn't try hard enough," Bethany adds.

"I'm kind of glad I didn't because Thomas and I finally had a chat, but I'm honestly not holding my breath for it to go my way. I think he is thinking of considering it, but the more that I think about it, the more I think he won't or shouldn't be with me."

"Why," asks Bethany.

"Because there are a lot of beautiful women out there, who are HIV free, and even if he says he is feeling me, I don't see him choosing me when there's better variety out there that he won't have to worry about."

"I see."

"Yes, I like him, but I have to be realistic. Why would he choose me?"

"Love has a funny way of making people look past the flaws. Maybe he is seeing you and not the virus."

I laugh at her statement. Maybe he is but, I doubt it. Nothing goes well in my life and I'm accepting that. Thomas will wake up and move on.

"What about the other guy, Jason is it?"

"Things with Jason were going well in the beginning, and he is positive like I am, but he slept with someone that I know, and when he told me that, I haven't spoken to him since. He still contacts me, but I will talk to him when I'm ready."

"Wait, Jason is positive, and you still have feelings for Thomas? So why are you upset with Jason," Bethany asks.

"Because I was willing to be with Jason. We are both going through something, and I thought we would be perfect together. We would support each other and just be happy. It's not all about the virus. The virus is part, but there are other things that we talk about and do together. I am crushing on Thomas, but I wasn't just going to stop with what was blossoming with Jason. Thomas is iffy and I'm not really sure about us, anyway."

"But you're willing to let Thomas in since Jason slept with a friend?"

"I don't know, but what I do know is that she sure isn't a friend. Whatever happens, I want it to happen naturally."

My phone rings. I pick it up to look at the caller ID and it's Jason. I sit the phone back down and look back at the screen.

"Do you need to--," Bethany starts, but I cut her off.

"Nope, it's fine. They can wait."

Then my doorbell goes off continuously and now my phone.

I jump to my feet. "On second thought, I think I need to cut this short. See you next week."

I close the laptop and rush downstairs. I see Jason is calling me, but who's at the door?

I ignore Jason's call and switch to the camera app, and there Jason is, standing at my door while trying to call me. I'm not ready to see him, so I let him ring on.

After fifteen minutes of Jason ringing the bell, I send him a text.

"Jason, can you please stop ringing my bell? I'm with my mom and your constant bell ringing is sending a ton of alerts to my phone!"

The constant ringing then turns to constant text messages.

"Vonne, please meet with me when you get home? I really want to work this out."

"There's nothing to work out. You were angry with me, and I get that, but to use it to be with Kia, I don't get. Be angry with me without sleeping with other women. Please, just stop texting me for right now."

I know more texts are coming, so I decide to mute him temporarily. I check the camera and I see him pull off. With my friends all at their jobs, it leaves me with nothing to do but think about this mess I'm in.

***

It's around 5 pm and after binge-watching reality tv shows all day, I get ready to head up north to Rita's coffee shop. This will be interesting since I know there will be questions because no one has seen me since Saturday, except for Ming.

I walk into a busy shop. This is the place to come to during the evening rush. I see my friends sitting at their usual table, and I take in a deep breath and sigh as I head over. I'm regretting coming here but I can't hide forever.

"Well, look who it is," says Cashmere, "Have a seat because I want to know why you left us all at the fair."

"Yeah, you left me with this crazy woman," Karma jokes.

"I was just ready to go," I say as I sit down.

"Something happened, didn't it," Cashmere asks with an added eye roll.

"Why do you think something happened?"

I don't want to talk about this right now, but I don't think these two are going to let me get away that easily.

"Come on you two," Ming jumps in, "she just got here!"

"I saw Thomas at the Couples Fair and I went to talk to him. Jason saw me and Thomas talking, so he went to hang with Kia alone in a corner and blamed me for being there with her. Then, I find out Sunday afternoon that he and Kia fucked. The end."

I just said everything so matter of fact because I wanted to get it out and hopefully move to another subject. Who am I kidding? I know damn well they aren't going to let this slide.

"What?!"

Karma and Cashmere silenced the entire shop for a minute before everyone resumes their activities.

"Yes, that's why I left. Jason was in a dark corner hugged up on Kia saying I couldn't say anything because I was talking to some guy."

Cashmere is quiet but fuming. When she gets quiet and doesn't say anything at all, is when I can tell she is going to the rage stage. And this is the person who laughs at anything, so seeing her rage stage is very rare.

"That bitch," Cashmere mumbles.

"Yeah."

"Wait, why are you so quiet," Cashmere asks Ming.

"Because I know already," Ming answers, "I went over to Vonne's house Sunday night."

"That's not all," I say. "Jason thought he would come clean and tell me Sunday, but saw Thomas leaving my house, and was livid."

"What," Cashmere and Karma exclaim in unison... again.

"Thomas was at your house," Cashmere asks. "Did you fuck him?"

I slap my face with my palm and shake my head while laughing.

"No, we didn't, and if we did, it's none of your beeswax."

"Wait, are you and Thomas okay now," Karma asks.

"I think so. He is a much better communicator in person."

I guess, like most men, Thomas isn't a phone person or a texter. I'm glad we finally had a conversation, but I'm still confused about his actions at my house.

"Hey, Rita, can I get a caramel hot chocolate?"

I look over to the counter, and there stands Kia. I hope she doesn't come her ass over here. I don't feel like dealing with her shit, but of course, she's coming our way. She gets her hot chocolate and over to our table she comes, her and her huge grin.

Ming is rolling her eyes while Cashmere is trying to stand up with Karma fighting to keep her seated.

"Why did you do it," I ask Kia.

Cashmere huffs. "Seriously, Vonne, you are wasting your breath."

"Why do you care, Vonnie, your attention was on some guy, and it looked pretty heated over there," Kia says as she giggles.

"So, I can't have a conversation!"

"Apparently not, since it put your guy in my bed," Kia retorts.

Cashmere rises from her seat, knocking Karma's resistant hand off her shoulder.

"Oh, hell no," she yells, "I've had enough of you."

"No, no, no," Karma says, "Do you remember where we are? A coffee shop."

"That's right," Ming adds, "and who loves coffee? The cops who are in and out of here. Sit down, Cashmere. Not here!"

Kia is sipping on her hot chocolate, still standing at our table with that stupid grin.

"Well, I can understand why you're upset, Vonnie, Vonne, Vonne," Kia says as she turns to walk out. "Your man has an enormous dick. If I were you, I would want to keep him to myself, too."

I feel my body temperature rise. I'm fuming, but I don't get up. My friends are all sitting at the table, wide-eyed at Kia's remark, staring at me.

"I think I'm going to head on home."

"Vonne--," Ming starts.

"Nah, I need to go." I gather my things and head for the door.

I rush out the door without looking back at the ladies or saying another word. I hope this bus is coming because I need to get out of here before I catch a case.

***

I get home and have a small meal alone, as usual. I have so much on my mind, and I can't make my brain shut the hell up. After the drama at the coffee shop, I'm thinking of just leaving Jason alone. Yeah, we are done!

It's about 10 pm and after having my bath, which I thought would make me feel better, it didn't. I get into bed and I'm getting ready to find a movie to fall asleep to when my phone pings.

I look, and it's a message from Thomas. He wants to come over tonight.

"Hi, Thomas, I just got in bed. Do you mind coming over in the morning?"

"I'm outside your door."

I hate when people come over unannounced, but I should be used to it since it's happening more frequently now. I get out of my bed and throw on a robe.

"I'm sorry to just drop by, but I need to talk to you now," says Thomas.

I invite him in, and we both have a seat on the sofa. I can't really read him, but I don't think this is anything good, and that's why I stop getting happy nowadays because nothing ever seems to go in my favor.

"It's fine. I can't seem to get to sleep anyway. What's going on?"

Thomas starts by clearing his throat. "I have been thinking about everything that we've talked about. I really like you but, I'm afraid that I can't be with you."

There is silence. I can feel tears rushing to my eyes and I try hard to fight them, but I can't stop the flow. I'm not mad at all. I'm a bit disappointed. I've fallen for this man before we ever met and the more, I communicated with him, my feelings grew stronger. Now I have to find a way to get my stubborn heart to let him go.

"Vonne--,"

"You don't need to say anything. This isn't your fault at all and I'm not angry."

He gently rests his hand on my thigh. "I don't want you to cry. I'm so sorry, Vonnie."

I slowly rise to my feet and wipe my face with the back of my hand. If I couldn't sleep before, I'm gonna have a hell of a time trying now.

"You're fine, Thomas. At least I got to meet one of my favorite actors," I say with a forced smile.

He gets up from his seat and grabs hold of both of my wrists. We look at each other, then I quickly turn away. I don't want him to feel bad and the tears are getting harder to stop.

"Vonne, I would like us to continue being friends."

"I'd like that too," I say softly in-between sniffles.

I pull my wrists away from his grasp and walk over to the door and open it. He follows behind me and as he steps outside, he turns to me and gives me a soft peck on my cheek.

"Good night, Vonne."

I give a slight wave. I can't speak. If I do, I will sob uncontrollably. I watch him as he gets in his car before I shut the door.

A few minutes later, there is a light tap on my door as I start away from it. I'm just thinking "maybe he left something". I wipe my eyes and I slowly open the door.

Thomas rushes in, grabs me, and pulls me close. Before I can react, his lips touch mine. I try to resist, but he is so strong as he swallows me up in his arms, I give in feeling needed. While we continue to share kisses, I feel myself being lifted, and he presses me against the front door, causing it to slam shut. I can't resist now that I'm pinned with my back firmly against the door and his body pressing on me securely with every kiss. I say nothing because I want him, but I can't help feeling like we shouldn't do this.

"Thomas, are you sure about this because I don't think we should—," I ask in between pecks.

"Very," he replies and begins again.

I force another interruption. I need to be certain. The last thing I want is him mad at me because we did something, and he later regrets it.

"I'm serious. You just told me you couldn't be with me."

"I can't — I don't know, maybe I do," he says, "but right now I just want you and I'm protected. Don't worry."

I want him too, so badly. But I can see he doesn't know if he wants to be with me. I told him the truth, and I just asked him if he was sure, so I think we are okay.

Thomas caresses my cheek with his lips as they slowly make their way down the slope of my neck, where he gently pinches me with a nibble that causes me to moan lightly.

Why is this happening? If he can't be with me, then why do this? I am so confused but my confusions are interrupted by Thomas' hands grabbing onto my hips firmly. His lips meet mine again. With my arms around his neck and my thighs clasped around his waist, my body press against his. I feel myself tremble. We both come up for air, and I look him in his dark brown eyes. I can see that he really wants this as much as I do just by the way he eyes me in return.

"Baby, you're fine," he whispers with a smile.

The bass of his voice as he reassures his affection sends chills up my spine. I say nothing, but my body wants more. I obey what my body is feeling and lean in to start our kissing session once more. After a few more pecks, Thomas carries me upstairs to my room.

7

HIV-Positive Vibes

"**Y**ou are cheating, Cash," Karma yells, "You have to draw four! I only saw you pick up three cards!"

Cashmere is laughing but isn't picking up the fourth card.

"I got four cards you just didn't see it."

"Yeah, okay, cheater," Karma says with giggles.

"Uno! I win," I yell, "and I won without cheating!"

It's a Friday night, and I asked the ladies to spend the weekend with me, because I just need it. All week, I have been down after the visit from Thomas. We chat and talk daily now, but we aren't together. Even after the night we had sex. He is now in Los Angeles for an interview and says he will see me tomorrow evening.

This isn't the first time a guy has wanted to just stay friends. Even after Thomas and I made love, we both agreed to be friends and see where it takes us. We talk a lot more now over the phone instead of on social media and he has visited since then. It's hard because when I'm around him, I just melt. I'm still in love with him and I can't seem to shake these feelings towards him.

Jason and I are still not talking. He still texts and comes by, but I always either ignore the door and texts or tell him to fuck off. Neither has been working.

Ming comes back from the liquor store and sits the bags down near the coffee table where we are playing the game 'Uno'.

"Pizza should be here shortly," Ming says.

"Oh, what did you get to drink," asks Karma while rummaging through the bags, getting the answer for herself.

"Shuffle and deal, Miss Cheat," I say to Cashmere as I'm tossing the cards over her way.

"So, what are you going to do about Jason, Vonne," Ming asks.

She sits down next to me and collects the cards being dealt.

"I'm not thinking about Jason at all. Why are you asking?"

"Well, because he's right outside," Ming answers, "I saw him sitting on the hood of his car as I came in."

We all fall silent. Cashmere puts the cards on the table and gets up from the floor.

"What are you doing," I ask Cashmere. "Get back here!"

She looks out the windows with not even a hint of subtlety, pulling the curtain back wide enough that I'm sure Jason can see us all in the living room clearly. I roll my eyes and get up. I'm going to have to talk to him because he just won't stop unless I do.

"You're going out there," Karma asks as she quickly rises and dashes to the window.

"Yes, I guess I am."

I slowly open the front door and step out onto the porch. I'm really not in the mood for this shit. With a heavy sigh, I make my way over to where Jason stands.

"Stalking? Really?"

"I just want us to talk," Jason pleads.

He looks tired, like he hasn't slept in days. He came to my house in his unmarked car. His partner isn't with him.

"I have nothing to say. You slept with someone else because you were mad at me. What if I piss you off again? Will you sleep with another woman?"

He hangs his head down low as if he is a sad puppy getting scolded for peeing the floor.

"I know, Vonne, I fucked up."

"Tell me, Jason, while you were fucking this trash whore, did you at least tell her that you are positive?"

"It never came up."

I scoff at his reply. "Oh, so you went right to business, then."

"Vonne--,"

"No! I'm still angry with you," I yell.

As I hear my voice rising, I tone it down to an angry whisper. I don't want a scene for my neighbors.

"I said I don't want to talk to you. Please leave me alone. If you want to talk, wait until I'm good and ready."

With that, I turn around and storm into the house, slamming the door. Every time I think of what Kia said to me at that coffee shop just pisses me off more and he trying to force a conversation isn't helping him.

"Is he still there," I ask Cashmere.

"Yeah, and the pizza just arrived," she answers, heading to the door.

I guess Karma knows the game is over because she collects the cards and puts them neatly back in the case.

***

"He looks so pitiful," says Cashmere with a mouth full, "Poor asshole."

"Yeah, well, he fucked this up, not me," I say right before taking a huge bite of my slice.

"Kia is such an — ugh," Ming shouts.

"Are you going to confront her again," Karma asks.

"Of course, she's not," says Cashmere while wiping away the sauce dripping from her mouth and chin, "That's why I'll be the one to confront her."

"Oh boy," Ming says before taking a sip of her drink.

"You guys, just leave it alone! I'm not going to jail over a guy, and neither should you."

Cashmere sighs heavily. "Girl, you're good, because that couldn't have been me."

"We know, Cash, we were at your wedding," I say with a forced chuckle.

"What about Thomas, would you kick her ass for him," Cashmere asks, "We all know that you love him more than Jason, anyway."

She's not wrong. I think if Kia were to go after Thomas, I would half-kill her ass. But I believe that if Thomas were to be with me and truly wanted only me, I wouldn't have to show my ass. Now, if it went down that way where Kia gets her talons into Thomas, I'd probably just let him go, too. No man is worth that much trouble.

"I don't know. I don't want to think about that."

"Find a movie," Karma demands, "something funny before I head to bed."

"It's after 10 and you want to watch tv," Cashmere asks.

"Well, yeah. I don't want to lay down on a full stomach," says Karma.

"I don't think I can sleep," I say as I'm grabbing another slice of pizza.

"Is it because Thomas is coming to see you tomorrow or because of your interaction with your stalker," Cashmere asks.

I laugh while rolling my eyes. I'm sure my friends can see me blushing. I can't wait to see Thomas. Even if we are only friends, I still get excited knowing he's coming to see me.

"Aww, look at that grin," Karma teases.

"I'm just not sleepy yet."

As we all sit and watch the movie, my mind is elsewhere. I'm not as down as I once was, but I'm not satisfied with my life either. I'm still single and alone. Jason wants back in, but I'm not forgiving him right now, and even if I do, I can never trust him again. I think Thomas isn't with me because of my status, but I also think he wants to be free to do what he wants, and that's fine. I hope he doesn't think I'm friends with benefits because I'm greedy and I want all or nothing.

***

"That's what you're wearing," Cashmere asks.

I decide to wear leggings, a short hoodie dress, and pull my hair into a top bun. I think I look ok.

"What's wrong with what I have on," I ask Cashmere.

"It's a little plain, don't you think? I mean Thomas is on his way back to Chicago to see you so I thought you would at least try to make an effort with your outfit."

"Girl, please," I say with a huff, "I only make an effort for my man, and he is not."

"I think you look fine," says Ming.

"What are we doing today," Karma asks.

"I really just want to do nothing," Cashmere answers, "Work has been hectic, and I wouldn't mind staying in and eating all of Vonne's food."

"Hey!"

"What, you have all the goodies here," Cashmere says with a chuckle.

"I don't mind doing nothing either," says Ming. "It's quiet here and I don't have to go off on my neighbor for her loud music."

"That's why I moved into a house," I say. "My neighbors were awful at my last place."

Aside from Cashmere eating all my food, I'm glad to be with my friends — my sisters, and even though I'm not in a relationship anymore, I'm more positive these days. I'm sure it will be short-lived.

"Terrell is coming to pick me up," says Karma. "He wants to go eat at that pizza place in Hyde Park."

"I am pizza'd out," I say.

"They have other things there to eat," says Karma. "I know he wants their pizza. I'll eat something else. The food is wonderful there. Just can't think of the name of the place."

"I know which one you're talking about," says Ming, "and they do have good food."

"What time is he coming," I ask.

"5 tonight."

"I think Thomas will be here around that time.

"What's for breakfast," Cashmere asks as she's plopping down on my sofa.

"Whatever in the kitchen that you fix," I answer.

"Really," Cashmere says with a huff, "We are guests here."

"Bullshit," I say with a loud chortle. "Keep thinking that, and your ass will starve."

We all bust out laughing, except Cashmere, of course.

"Let's go to Rita's place," Karma suggests. "She has good pancakes. Better than the pancake shop."

"Um, did you forget about the part about us not going anywhere," Cashmere asks. "That's all the way up north!"

"I don't think Rita works today," I say. "Her son takes over on the weekends now unless she's bored."

Cashmere continues to look my way, as if she's waiting for me to offer to make breakfast.

"Well, McDonald's has pancakes," I suggest, "and I don't care what no one says. That syrup is the shit!"

"Yeah, it's down the street," says Karma, "I'll go get us breakfast."

"I'll take pancakes, hash browns, sausage, and eggs," I say with a grin, "with extra syrup."

"Damn, girl," Cashmere exclaims, "are you pregnant?"

Ming laughs. "Hell, I want the same thing."

"Okay, I'll just get everyone that," Karma says as she grabs her car keys and heads for the door.

I'm starving. Even after all that pizza I had last night. And no, I'm not pregnant. I can't believe they would ask me such a thing.

Karma opens the front door to leave but stops dead in her tracks. We all get up together to see what's outside.

"What is it," Ming asks while walking up to the door.

Cashmere is next to go see what's going on and I follow behind.

"Well, shit," Cashmere exclaims, "was his ass here all night?!"

I look to see Jason still at my house, but this time he is in his own car.

"No. He may have just got here. That's a different car than last night."

Ignoring Jason, I go back inside. He is getting on my nerves now.

"Okay, well, see you all in a bit with yummies," Karma says cheerfully.

Ming shuts the door behind her.

"What the hell, Vonne," asks Ming while shaking her head in disbelief. "Seriously, that guy has a problem."

"I'm going to go talk to him. The last thing I need is for him to be here when Thomas shows up."

I open the front door and slowly walk out before closing it behind me. I see Jason sitting on the driver's side with his seat leaned back. It looks like he is asleep, but he isn't. I go over on the passenger side and let myself into his car.

"What the hell, Jason?"

He doesn't answer. He just sits there like he is deep in thought. I'm feeling myself get nervous. Why did I get in this damn car? What if he takes me somewhere and kills me?

"Jason?!"

He slowly turns my way and looks at me. He has his hands in his pockets and I'm not liking that at all.

"Answer me, damn it!"

I reach for the door to leave, and that's when I feel a tight grip on my upper arm.

"I'm sorry," Jason starts, "I'm just... I don't know... you won't talk to me."

"I'm here now, so talk!"

He sits up and raises the driver's seat to its default position.

"I know what I did was wrong, and there is no excuse for it. I'm really sorry, Vonnie."

"I know, but I can't trust you.

"Are you with someone else," Jason asks.

"No, I'm not. The guy that you saw wants nothing to do with me romantically, but we are friends."

He lets out a soft sigh.

"Listen, Jason, all of this extra shit you're doing is freaking me out, and it's only making me want to stay away from you. This will not make me come back to you. You need to give me time."

"I know and I'm sorry for this. I just really wanted to see you, but I'll step back."

"Thank you. It's all I'm asking."

He looks away from me and falls silent again. I just sit there looking at him. I was really feeling him and was going to give us a try. Even if it meant to slowly put Thomas on the back burner. What he did was foul and I'm not forgiving. At least not now.

"Well, I guess I'm going to go," says Jason.

"I'm going to head on back inside. Please enjoy the rest of your day, Jason."

I open the door, and before stepping out of the car, I turn to look at him. He looks so down and tired. I sigh as I get out and close the door. I can feel him watching me as I'm walking past the front of his car until I get inside and shut the door.

Cashmere and Ming are standing near the window, and I know they were watching. I don't even think they care that I know.

"Everything okay," Ming asks.

"Yeah, everything is fine, but he just seems so down."

"They always do when they cheat," says Cashmere while rolling her eyes and scoffing.

"I don't know, you guys, maybe I should just take him back."

"What about Thomas," Ming asks.

"We made love one time, and he said that he didn't want to be in a relationship."

I can't tell Ming the full story while Cashmere is sitting here. They both give me a look of shock. Ming mouths something to me while Cashmere is focusing on me, but I can't make out what she is saying. I think I know, though.

"Wait, you and Thomas slept together," Cashmere asks.

"Yes, and I would really appreciate it if you said nothing when he gets here."

Then the bell rings. It must be Karma back with the food. Good, because I'm starving, and I really want to change the subject. I get up to let her inside.

"Did something happen," Karma asks, "because I don't see Jason outside anymore."

"No, nothing bad. We just had a little talk."

Karma sits the bags down on the coffee table, and I rush to see which is for me. We eat in silence; I think because we are all hungry. I turn the tv on and a court show is playing, and that's where I leave it.

"Oh, Rita called me while I was out," says Karma, "and she wants us to come by the shop and try her maple muffins. She is thinking of adding them on her menu."

"Well, I can be there after work," says Cashmere.

"Same," says Ming.

"Well, I don't have a job, so I guess I can too," I say. "I'll just see you guys after you all get off."

"We should all pitch in and help Vonnie get a car," says Karma, "I hate when you leave the north side alone on the bus."

"I know, but with a fixed income and only doing a few heads or nails at a time, how can I afford the upkeep, insurance, and gas?"

"Come work in my office," Ming suggests, "You can answer phones part time."

"I have been thinking about going back to work full-time. I miss it, but I'll have to ask my doctor about anxiety and depression medications to get me up and out the house and around people again without having a panic attack."

Cashmere stuffs the last piece of her pancake in her mouth and let out this enormous sound.

"I can't with you, Cash," I say, looking disgusted. "You have no home training."

We all laugh while Cashmere's burps continue.

"So, are you going to work as a pharmacy technician again," Ming asks.

"I'm thinking about it. There is a small pharmacy in my neighborhood that is hiring. They need more help now that the pharmacy chain we had closed and went to another area."

"Oh, I forgot to tell y'all, Kia has found an apartment on the north side and has a job at the—."

"Corner of 47th and Cicero," Cashmere asks, cutting in.

I laugh so hard that I almost choke on my food.

Ming laughs also while rolling her eyes. "No, she works for the 'Triton," she says, still laughing. "You know, the huge online store that delivers groceries and things from their website."

"Good for her, I guess," I say. "Maybe she will stay busy and stop messing with people."

We continue to eat our food, except Cashmere, who's done and flipping through the tv to see what else is on. A murder documentary appears on the screen after going through the channels and she settles for that, and we all watch attentively.

***

It's later in the day, and Terrell and Karma have left for dinner. Cashmere is going through my closet, insisting I change clothes for Thomas' arrival. Ming is asleep in my stiletto chair, snoring loudly, unbothered with Cashmere's loud mouth.

"Please put this on, Vonne," Cashmere demands.

She may have said please, but it was more like an order.

"I'm fine with what I have on. Now stop it!"

"Okay, but you like him. Maybe you should dress a little hotter so he will be more interested."

I laugh as I walk over to the closet and go through the clothes with her.

"Clothes have absolutely nothing to do with it, Cash."

Still wearing my long hoodie and leggings, I await Thomas' arrival. He should be here any minute. Cashmere finally gives up on looking for an outfit and we both head downstairs, leaving Ming to her nap.

"What do you and Thomas have planned," Cashmere asks.

"I'm not sure, but I'll just be happy to see him."

Right as I say that, the doorbell rings. I go to answer it, hoping it's Thomas and not Jason. I think I have a bit of PTSD after all the frequent stalking.

"Hey, Vonnie," Thomas says as I step back to let him inside.

We hug each other tight. The way we are holding each other right now, I'd say he missed me. If the girls weren't here, I have a feeling that hug would've turned into something more.

I take his jacket and hang it in the nearby closet and can't help but to look at him. He has on a pair of slacks with polo top. His beard is gone, and he shaved his head. I love him in his beard, but I can't tell him that because — I don't think it's my place since we aren't together.

"Hey, how was your flight back," I ask him.

"It was alright just glad to be back in Chicago," Thomas answers.

We both walk over to the sofa, where Cashmere is already sitting. Thomas chooses the chair, and I sit beside Cashmere.

"Is Ming and Karma here," asks Thomas.

"Karma is with Terrell and Ming is snoozing upstairs," says Cashmere.

"Do you want a water or something, Thomas," I ask.

"Nah, I'm good. Thanks."

I hear Ming at the top of the stairs, and she is on her way down. She still looks as if she is trying to wake up.

"So, Thomas, when are you and Vonne going to start dating," ask Cashmere. "I mean, I know you are both into each other, so cut the shit!"

I look over at Cashmere with mouth and eyes wide open. That got Ming more alert, and when I look over at Thomas, he looks back at me, smirking.

"Cash, stop it," I say in an annoyed whisper and add a pinch on her arm to let her know I'm serious.

"Do you need to be put in timeout, Cash," Ming asks with a giggle.

"I'm just saying, you can tell they are feeling each other. They need to just go ahead and be with one another."

Remember, Cashmere and Karma don't know that I am HIV positive, so I can't really explain the situation between Thomas and me.

"Cash, you're doing it again," Ming says as she makes herself comfortable on the area rug near the coffee table.

Thomas clearly looks uncomfortable but keeps smiling. I'm getting upset with Cashmere because she always does this, and we talked about that last summer when she and Ming got into it. I guess she will never learn.

"Well, ladies, I wanted to ask if you all would like to go to Navy Pier. They are having a dance and you must be in costume."

"Ooh, that sounds like fun," Cashmere says giddily with excitement.

I don't know if I want to go. Everyone will have dates, and Jason and I are no longer together. I can feel myself become a bit dishearten. I know Thomas is free and he may bring a date with him. Maybe it will be nice to go, besides dressing up is fun.

"We can meet up this coming Saturday," says Thomas.

"That's good," Ming says, "we are all off on weekends."

I'm looking for work and I filled out a few applications online. Maybe I will have the weekend off, but if not, then it will be a good thing. I don't have a date, anyway.

"Great," Thomas says as he claps his hands and rises from his seat. "I'll see you all on Saturday!"

I stand up quickly to walk him to the door.

"Are you leaving, Thomas," I ask.

"No, but can I speak with you for a minute?"

"Yeah, sure."

I lead him into the kitchen, leaving Ming and Cashmere with confused looks on their faces.

"What's up," I ask him.

"How have you been?"

"I've been okay. How was your trip?"

"Business as usual. You know I'm a hustler."

I smile but try not to flirt or give him any signals. I want to respect his decision but can't get over the night we were together and just want to pull him over and kiss him.

"You look like you want to tell me something, Thomas."

"I just want to look at you. Believe it or not, I've missed you."

"Don't. You made your decision, and I don't want to believe there is hope for us when you aren't ready to be with someone like me."

"I know," Thomas says, "but I can't help how I feel about you."

This is torture. He knows how I feel about him. Sometimes I just wish he would honor his decision and leave me alone. Okay, maybe not leave me alone, but not do this. Telling me constantly he is into me but doesn't want to be with me.

"Okay, I'll get going," Thomas says, "but I'll see you soon, You look great by the way."

With that compliment, I can't help but think back on Cash criticizing my outfit. Told you, Cashmere.

"Thanks," I say with a smile. "Let me walk you out."

We make our way through the living room where Cashmere and Ming still sit, looking at tv, and finally to the front door.

"Drive safe," I say to him.

"Be good."

We hug tightly except this time, there is an added kiss on my cheek. He takes a small step back and places his finger under my chin, causing me to look up at him. I look into his eyes, and they are telling me one thing, and it's not what he has decided about us.

"Thomas," I say in a whisper.

He takes a deep breath and acts as if he's coming out of a trance. I see that this is torture for him as well. He caresses my cheek before quickly looking away from me.

"Good night, Vonnie."

He turns and walks out the door as if he may have made some sort of mistake. I'm not sure if that mistake is the decision of us not being together or what happened the night we made love.

I close the door with a heavy sigh. It feels awful when you love someone and can't be with them. I'm trying not to go back into depression, but this suck.

"Everything alright," Ming asks.

"Yeah, I guess," I answer.

I walk over to the sofa and sit. I think my friends can tell that I'm down, but they are silent. Ming gets up from the floor and sits next to me on the sofa and just holds me. I try not to cry, but the tears are flowing, and I say nothing.

"I hate this," Cashmere says, "Why aren't you two together? It's so obvious that he's into you and you him."

"I think I'm going to go lay down."

I get up from the sofa as I'm wiping my tears away and head upstairs. I just hate this so much that sometimes I want to just end this life and see if I can start over.

Once in my room, I lay down and stare at the ceiling. My thoughts are busy with every moment that was spent with Thomas. Perhaps I should take a break from him. The dance at the pier sounds like a lot of fun, but I will be miserable there. I just know it.

8

I'm Sorry

On Monday morning, I get ready for a job interview. I am excited yet nervous and I wonder if I should go on with it. I haven't had a job in years and I'm 37 years old.

I haven't heard from Thomas since Saturday and that's fine. I think I need a break from him because I am torturing myself, but wait, I see him this Saturday at the Navy Pier. Maybe after that I will stay away. Hopefully, I am hired, and I can focus on the job instead of him.

I heard from Jason, well, a text asking me how I was doing and that he misses me. I didn't reply.

All dressed and ready, I head downstairs and start a fresh cup of coffee. I'm not hungry, so this will be breakfast. I look over my resume and put it back in my bag, grab my keys, and head to the interview.

When I arrive, I look at the building. It's small, old and is standing alone with vacant lots on both sides. It looks like it needs work, but hey if I get the job, at least it's close to home.

After making my way inside, I see there are 4 rows of seats in the waiting area, which are all full. It's pretty busy. There are kids running around while their mothers call for them and scold them, crying babies, coughing patients. I guess this is me now, hopefully.

There is a line of patients waiting their turn to get their prescriptions filled. I wait in line as if I am waiting too except; I need to talk to someone about my interview.

Finally, my turn. My stomach is doing flip-flops, and I'm about ready to turn around and leave. I keep telling myself that this can help me. Something to keep my mind on, not the other things going on in my life.

"Hi, I'm Yvonne Dent and I am here for an interview."

"One sec," says the woman at the counter.

She is a heavyset woman who is chewing loudly on gum and popping it, also loudly. She goes in the back for something, so I thought, except she comes out to the counter with an older man. Looks to be Pakistani or I don't know, maybe somewhere from the Middle East.

"Welcome, Yvonne," the man says with a smile. "I am Manjeet, the pharmacist here, and I will be the one interviewing you today. Please follow me."

His accent isn't too rich as it is easy to understand him. He walks with a slight limp, short and very thin. He has white hair but a salt and pepper beard.

We enter a small room. It almost looks like an exam room but without the exam table. It has the sink and a storage cabinet. There is also a small table that looks pretty old, with four seats. The walls are dingy and make the room look very dull and depressing.

"Please have a seat," he says as he chooses his seat and also sits.

He puts down a file he carried into the room with him. I can only guess that it must be my information. While he is going over the filled application, I sit quietly while listening to the chaos going on in the waiting room.

"It says here that you haven't been working since 2001, yes?"

"That is correct."

"May I know why," Manjeet asks.

"Well, I have some medical issues that caused me to be on disability.

"Are you able to work now? You will be on your feet most of the day and it is an eight-hour shift."

"Yes. It isn't a physical disability."

"I see that you have your degree here, but are you licensed? It is a requirement."

"Yes, I am. When I started applying for pharmacy positions, I made sure to get retested for my license since it has been a while and I've done refresh studies at home to bring me up to speed, however, there are a lot of new medicines now and I don't have those in my books that I used back when I was studying."

"That's fine, that's fine. What did you do in your last job?"

"On my last job, I prepared, labeled, and filled prescriptions, answered phones, and gave injections, like flu shots, for example."

"The pay is 9.50 an hour and the hours are from 8 am to 4 pm with the pharmacy closing at 12 pm for lunch, Monday through Friday," Manjeet says as he put my paperwork back into the file.

"Are you saying I got the job," I ask.

"If you want it. If so, I'll go get the paperwork for you to fill out for the background and drug test."

"Yes," I answer. "Thank you!"

He nods and leaves the room. I sit waiting, but I am so nervous. As I said, I haven't worked in years.

"Here you are," Manjeet says as he hands me the papers and walking back out.

After filling out the applications for drug testing and background check, I return to the front desk to give back the signed papers. We shake hands and I leave. I feel like I've accomplished something. I'm opening back up to life slowly but surely and it feels awesome! Still a single woman, but for right now, it's fine. I do wish that Thomas and I were together, but I accept that we aren't, well, as long as he stops making googly eyes at me when we see each other.

***

After a day of good news, I decide I want to tell the girls at the coffee shop. That's usually the spot for when Ming, Karma, and Cashmere go to unwind from a busy day. And now, I will be doing the same. Well, I don't know because all three live nearby and I am on the far south side. Maybe, my next task is finally to buy a car.

I walk in and I can hear Cashmere shushing everyone and I'm thinking what are they up to now.

"Hey, ladies," I say happily, with a wide grin.

"Hey, you," says Karma, "get over here and sit."

As I take my seat and get ready for what they are up to because of all the hush-hush, I see the maple muffins that Rita wants us to try. They smell so good that the scent is changing the status of my appetite since I didn't have one earlier. I want to share my news first, so I put whatever they are hiding to the side for now.

"Guess what?"

"What," asks all three in unison.

I sat there with a grin, letting about a minute go by before telling them about my day.

"I am officially a Pharmacy Technician!"

"Oh my god," Cashmere says with excitement, "are you for real?"

"Okay, it's not official yet, but I know I got it because I have no drugs in my system and my background is clean, so I am optimistic that I will be official soon."

"Congratulations," says both Karma and Ming.

"I'm thrilled for you," Cashmere adds.

"Thanks, ladies," I say, still grinning, "but why are you shushing one another as I am walking up to you? What's going on?"

"Well, I bought a new car, and I thought that you should have my old one," Ming says.

"Really," I ask while still grinning, "I was just saying to myself that I needed a car."

"Yup," Ming answers.

She hands me the keys, and I take them graciously. I look at them and I feel myself getting a little emotional. Not only because Ming gave me her car, but because I have so many people around me that look out for me and often, I am thinking of quitting.

Ming puts her arm around me and gives me a hug. "Hey, are you okay?"

"I'm just having a good day, that's all."

"Aw, you know we love you, girl," Karma says. "Cash told me what happened when Thomas was at your house the night me and my husband were out for dinner. It will get better."

I don't want to go back to that night. So, I turn the conversation back to the job.

"Well, I don't have the job yet, but as soon as I can, I'll get insurance and things to make sure I'm all legal to drive."

The car that Ming is giving to me is a "Kia" SUV. Yeah, funny right? But it's something to get around in and I am grateful.

"Thank you so much, Ming," I say as I stand up to hug her. "I really appreciate this."

"I parked the car at my house," Ming says, "so when you are ready to get it, it's there."

"Don't look now," Karma says after a long loud gasp, "Jason is here, and he isn't alone."

You know we all turned to see who was with him, naturally. Sure enough, there is Kia on his arm as if they are a thing. Am I upset? No, not at all. What I see here is karma brewing because the four of us, Kia's family, and almost the whole west side of Chicago, know how Kia runs and Jason is nothing special. In fact, Kia is only showing out because he and I used to date. I think it's funny and sad at the same damn time.

As both Kia and Jason walk up to Rita, who is at the counter with a look of stun, I can't help but to bust out in laughter. My laughter is so loud that the entire coffee shop looks directly at our table. Kia looks at me with a smirk on her face. I guess she thought I would come out of character, but no, I know it won't last long before she hops on someone else's dick. I'm telling you; Jason needs to worry about Kia, especially when she meets his brother.

Then there is Jason. He seems to be emotionless. I can't get a read on him, but if I had to guess, I would say that he is either relieved that I am not confronting them or surprised that I didn't.

Rita is looking at me with raised eyebrows and seems to be uncomfortable.

"Um, sweetie," Ming starts, "are you okay?"

Still chortling, I reply, "I am fine. I can't wait to see how this goes."

Now, I'm not saying that because I want to get back at Jason... okay, maybe I am, but I don't want him to hurt. I know it hurt me when he told me what he did. I guess I just want to see how this ends up because we all know that Kia is not looking for anything monogamous.

"I'm fine," I answer again since my friends can't stop staring at me.

"Wow, just wow." Cashmere exclaims. "He was just stalking you and begging you to forgive him, and now he's with her again? The bitch who started this?"

"Calm down, Cash," I say, "It's fine. Really."

"Well, I hope you are really okay," Ming says, "because here he comes."

"What," I say while turning back to look at the counter.

Sure enough, Jason is on his way. I don't know why the hell for because I meant it when I said that I am done.

"Hi, Vonne, can we talk," Jason asks.

"No, there is really nothing to talk about, Jason."

"I tried to give you a chance to come back to me, but you wouldn't' so I am moving on."

"What an asshole," Cashmere blurts out.

"Okay. Not sure why you needed to come tell me that. I wish you the best of luck."

"Because you're gonna need it," Cashmere adds.

"What does that supposed to mean, Cash," Jason snaps.

"Your answer will come soon enough," Cashmere shot back.

He looks at all of us for a minute, then just at me.

"I'm really sorry that I hurt you, Vonne," he says before turning and walking back over to Kia.

"Wow," Ming says as she is shaking her head in disbelief.

"It's fine, guys."

It did hurt a little when they walked in together. I wasn't ready to go back to Jason because of his cheating and then to cheat out of anger instead of talking about it didn't help either. So, just like that, the two men that I thought I would have something with turned into nothing and I am back to where I started. Single.

"Well. you guys, I think I am going to head on home," I say as I collect my belongings and grab a muffin.

"Okay, Vonnie," Ming says, "Meet us here on Friday so that we can shop for our costumes for Saturday and make sure you call or text us when you get in."

"I will."

I turn and wave to everyone at our table. I look at both Jason and Kia. They look back at me, but Jason quickly turns away. One last wave to my friends, before walking out of the shop as I am shaking my head.

***

"I hope your costume will be better than that outfit," Cashmere says.

"Mind your business." I say back to Cashmere.

"Ooh, maybe I can be a sexy witch," Karma exclaims.

"Sexy is all because you don't fit the character of a witch," I say. "That's more Cashmere."

We all double-over laughing except for Cashmere, who's just mockingly mouthing what I've just said and rolling her eyes.

"Be right back, ladies," I say as I hurry away.

I leave the group because there is a costume that I can see myself in and I don't want the girls to grab it. Am I wrong?

What I'm eyeing is a beautiful flesh-tone Cleopatra costume that has a beaded headband-like crown and halter maxi dress with high splits on both sides. The thin strings of glitter and sparkles are placed in both splits. I am so glad I like to save money because if I didn't, I wouldn't be able to buy it. Then I look at the price tag and sigh. It says 89.00 written on a small brown tag in blue ink. What the hell. I'm still getting it. But then I see that the blunt block fringe bang wig is separate at 39.00. Of course, I must have it too, so I grab the wig head with the wig still on it along with the costume and walk it over to the saleswoman nearby to make my purchases.

Ming walks over and starts inspecting my soon-to-be costume on the counter.

"Oh, this is nice," she says as she is petting the fabric of the maxi dress, "You will definitely turn heads in this get-up."

"I hope not," I say with a light laugh, "because my heart is for one man even if he doesn't want to be with me."

"I think he does," Ming declares. "He shows it by how he looks at you. Saturday, you didn't notice, but when I came downstairs and you, him, and Cash were talking, he had his eyes on you from then until you both went into the kitchen. I think he has fallen hard for you, and he may end up being with you whether you both know it or not."

"I don't know, Ming, because even if he has feelings for me, he won't date me. Yeah, we had a moment and had sex a little time after, but I'm not seeing us together."

I don't want to get my hopes up, but Ming seems to think that we will be together, eventually. He is 57 years old, there is not a lot of time, and I don't want him to decide when he's 70.

"Have you decided on a costume," I ask. I really want to change the subject.

"No, still looking. But Cashmere is getting the tight cat suit with a tail and Karma really wants that witch costume."

"Let me ask the saleswoman to hold my items and we can look for you a costume and me some shoes."

With that, we walk off to look at the many costumes the busy store offers. Oh, I forgot to mention—they hired me at the pharmacy, so now I am a working girl again. Yay! Not only that, but it feels good to not be on the bus thanks to my bestie, Ming. I was able to get the insurance for the SUV with savings and I can't wait to go visit my mom and aunt after we leave here.

As I'm looking around the store, I'm thinking what costume is a good fit for Ming and her personality? She is rather reserved, but she has a sense of humor which is good, so I don't want to pick something that she won't feel comfortable with yet something too dull either.

"I see something I think you will like, Ming," I say as I'm walking over to a beautiful fairy display near the back of the store.

"What is it?"

"Come here," I demand. "Come and see it!"

It is so beautiful. A fairy costume, green with a light-yellow hue and subtle, but noticeable hints of sparkling glitter on the knee-length skirt of the tulle dress. The wings are green with yellow tones and full of glitter. I think Ming will like it.

"Gosh," Ming exclaims, "this is perfect, but I don't know if I want the wings."

"Why? It goes perfectly with the dress and the shoes are cute too."

The shoes are a clear tinted yellow color with a high heel and close by; I see a tiara. Ming sees me eyeing it and immediately jumps in front of my view.

"I don't think so, Vonne. It's too much!"

"Let's see what Karma and Cash think."

After calling the two over, Karma is immediately in awe while Cashmere looks to be studying it as if the costume is under inspection.

"I think Vonne is right," Cashmere says while still looking at the costume. "This suits you, Ming."

"Try it on," Karma demands, "let's see how it looks on you."

"Alright, alright." Ming gives in and picks up the dress and wings before heading to the dressing room.

"Is this you," Cashmere asks.

She is looking at my Cleopatra costume on the counter.

"Yup! I just need to find some shoes to go with it and maybe an anklet with armbands."

Cashmere shakes her head while giggling. "Oh, you're going to be hot! Thomas is going to take one look at you and probably propose."

I laugh as I am shaking my head. If this costume gets me married to Thomas, then I'll pay Cashmere for the hook-up. After all, she was the one that tried to push us together last Saturday. I'm being realistic here. No clothes will get a guy to marry you. My crazy mouthy friend is just joking around.

While Ming tries on the fairy costume, I decide to use the time and find some shoes for mine. I see a pair of clear plastic high-heels and because they are clear, they will go perfectly with my costume. The anklets I see look simple and they are gold. They sparkle in the light and don't cost much. These may turn green after a while but it's for my costume, so I don't care.

I hear Karma and Cashmere in awe when Ming walks out of the changing room. I hurry over to see her and she is stunning! Even without the shoes, the costume is perfect. The light gives Ming a nice sparkle, and the green fits her olive skin tone. Karma sneaks over and adds the tiara and then there is perfection. Ming says I'll be turning heads. I think she has me beat.

"It's beautiful, bestie," I say as I'm walking around her to check every inch of the costume that I hope she decides on.

"Okay, I love it, but I'm not wearing the Wings."

"Why," we all ask simultaneously.

"Because, it's a dance! I don't want people getting upset with me because my wings are bumping into them. These are huge!"

"I think the wings make the costume," I say. "If they don't want to get hit, then they should stay away."

"Hi, Ms., my friend will be getting this fairy outfit," Cashmere says as if she didn't care about Ming's decision.

"Okay, I will purchase it, but I'm telling you all right now, if that place is packed, the wings come off."

Ming heads back into the dressing room to change into her clothes, and I'm ready to check out. I want to visit my mom and aunt before it gets too late.

"Okay, ladies," I say as I grab the shoes and jewelry to go with my costume, "I am going to go pay for these and then head over to my mom and aunt's house."

"Okay, Vonne Vonne," Karma says cheerfully, "be safe and tell them I said hello."

I pay for my things and hug everyone except Ming, who is still changing back in the dressing room.

"I'll call you all later," I say as I am heading towards the exit.

***

The drive is pleasant, but short. A tremendous difference than being on the bus. Why did I wait so late to drive? This is awesome!

"Hey, baby, I've missed you," my mom says, and she's squeezing me like a stuffed animal.

"Hi, Mama and Auntie," I greet as I'm returning affections.

"What's been going on," my aunt asks.

"I got a job," I say, smiling.

"And you are driving now," my mom asks.

"Yeah. Ming was nice to give me her old car after she bought a new one."

"What about your social security," my mom asks.

"I called, and they said I have a 9-month trial and I have to report my earnings monthly, but I think I am ready to get back out there and not let my life waste away, anymore."

"That's good, honey. How are you and what's his name?"

Oh boy. I haven't told my mom or aunt about the drama that has unfolded with me and Jason, and when she finds out that Kia is involved, their responses may be harsh. Even for god-fearing women.

"Well, you guys, Jason and I are no longer together. He cheated on me with Kia and now they are dating."

"Kia. the one who slept with her mom's husband or something," my mom asks.

"Her boyfriend, and yes, that's her."

"Wow, sounds like she needs Jesus in her life," my aunt says.

"Nah, she would probably just fuck him too," I say casually.

"Language, missy," my mom scolds.

"It's the truth!"

My mom gives me a look that lets me know she is serious.

"You hungry," my mom asks.

"Yeah, what did you cook?"

"I made cabbage, baked chicken, cornbread, and mac and cheese," she answers as she goes into the kitchen to fix me a plate.

"I miss your cooking. I think I hear my tummy agreeing with me with the low growls."

"You miss your mama, huh," my auntie asks with a grin, "Well, you can't have her because she is good company."

"I wouldn't take her from you, Auntie. Just her food."

We both laugh.

"Here you are, sweetie," my mom says as she's handing me a plate.

The food smells good, like it's a Sunday or Thanksgiving Day. My plate is full. I think she may want me to stay the night, but I need to get ready for tomorrow. I want to put out some Halloween decorations before I leave for the dance.

"This is good, Mama," I say will a mouth full of food.

"Have you been eating well," my mom asks with a perplexing look on her face.

"Yeah. Mostly prepared frozen meals."

"Why," asks my aunt, "when you can cook."

"It's just me."

"So, you can make enough for yourself and if any is left, save it."

"Oh, Auntie, I doubt I will do any cooking now that I am working,"

I'm enjoying spending time with my mom and aunt. I miss my mom. She used to be there when I leave the house and say her "I love yous" and have good food cooked. I really need to visit them more.

"Are you still talking with your therapist," my mom asks.

"I tried it like you suggested, but I missed my last session. Don't think I'm going to continue."

"Why did you stop?"

"Because it's doing the opposite of helping, Mom," I say with a heavy sigh. "It's supposed to help me but it's making me more depressed."

"I don't want you to give up so easily, honey."

"I know, Mama, but it's just not for me."

My mom knows about my situation, and I have been wondering when or if I should tell my aunt. It's just the three of us left in our family, at least I think it is. My mom's side is all I know and my grandparents both passed away from a horrible food bourne illness. The only sisters I have are my friends. My father wants nothing to do with me, so I don't even know anyone on that side.

"Thanks for dinner, Mama. I need to get going. The girls and I have plans tomorrow."

"What do you have planned," my mom asks.

"Right," my aunt adds while chuckling, "She got herself a car and now she has plans."

I laugh and roll my eyes. "We are going to Navy Pier. I am trying to get out again and so far, it's been nice."

"I'm glad to see that, sweetie," my mom says as she pulls me into a hug.

I give my aunt a hug too before going into their kitchen and stealing me a plate of food to take home for later.

"Okay, fam, I'm leaving."

"Drive safely, Yvonne," my mom says sternly, with a worried look on her face. "You are new at this."

"I'll call when I get home."

***

On my way home, I can't help but wonder what Thomas is doing. I think about him a lot and I shouldn't be. What if he brings someone to the masked dance with him? Then my thoughts move to "Am I ready to pay those high ass parking prices downtown?" Maybe I'll catch the bus, I don't know.

I call my mom to let both her and my aunt know I made it in safely. I miss my mom, but it's nice to have the house to myself.

"Hello?"

I decide to call Ming to see if anyone is driving downtown.

"Hey, Ming, I just need to know how everyone is going to Navy Pier."

"Karma and Cash are taking the bus, but I am going to drive."

"Yeah, I was thinking of taking the bus, too. The parking prices downtown are insane! And some charge a butt-load an hour and I cannot afford that."

"Well, I guess I'll bus it too, but, we are all on the north side and you're the only one coming from out south. Do you feel comfortable traveling alone all dressed up?"

"I have been riding the bus all of my life," I say with a laugh. "I will be fine."

"Ask Thomas to pick you up. I'm sure as hell he wouldn't be caught dead on public transportation."

She might be right, but some actors aren't against taking public transportation, are they? Well, if he does or not, I am not asking him a damn thing. I am trying to stick to being buddies as much as possible and I don't want my feelings hurt because we are together. I get all caught up in my feels very easily. We both said that we should be friends, but our minds don't seem to wanna honor that mutual decision.

"Not gonna happen, Ming," I say with a groan.

"Well, please be careful, Vonnie. I love you."

"I will. Love you too and see you guys tomorrow."

***

I wake up to a text from Thomas asking me if I'm still going to the pier. I reply "yes", and he sends a 'smile' emoji.

After showering, I decide to try on my costume. Why I didn't do this in the store, I don't know, but I want to see how it looks on me. It's a good thing I didn't try it on in the store because if this costume makes me look as hot as I think it will, I'll get that "wow" when I show up.

Speaking of "wow" when I step in front of my floor-length mirror on my closet's sliding door, I am in awe of myself. This costume is beautiful and now I cannot wait to go to the dance to have fun and feel gorgeous! I have been a recluse for years until recently last summer, and to finally come out and enjoy life, feels so good. I do still get depressed at times, but now, I just try to do things to help me cope. I may give therapy another try if she can see me on the weekends, since I am working now.

As I'm finishing applying my makeup, the doorbell rings. I am not expecting anyone, and Jason and I haven't spoken since the coffee shop.

"Wow! You look gorgeous!"

It's Karma, and she looks like a sexy witch. In fact, she looks like a good witch. Karma has a sweet personality, and I just don't think the witch costume fits her, but I guess that's why people dress up for Halloween, to become something they are not. She is still rocking the costume, though.

"Girl, you might end up leaving the party with a man," says Karma as she is touching my wig and jewel headband.

"Thank you," I say with an enormous smile.

"I'm going to leave my car here and we can Uber together when the party ends or when we leave."

"That's fine, Karma," I say while fixing my wig.

"What time do you think we should leave? You know the bus schedule better than any of us. Wait, no, Cashmere knows too. She drives them for a living."

"I think we should leave at about 6 because there may be traffic, but I mean we don't have to be there right on time, do we?"

Karma looks at the time on her phone and I look at the clock sitting on the side table. It is only 3 pm. We have a lot of time to kill.

"Okay well, let's take pictures for the 'MediaPal'," Karma demands.

As sexy as I look and feel, I can't wait to show off for the camera. Karma starts first, and I take her pictures.

Her poses are innocent, almost like how a shy girl would pose. Come on, girl, you're a witch. Act like it!

"That's not very witchy," I say with a laugh.

She gives me a fake miserable look with a pout before laughing at herself.

"Okay, Vonne, your turn."

I make sure I pose very provocatively. My dress has slits on both sides going up to my hips. I'm purposely giving a lot of leg. I haven't had a photoshoot in a while for my 'MediaPal' account and I'm truly enjoying this. Feels like I'm making a comeback into life.

"You better get it, girl," says Karma as she is acting like a professional photographer. Sometimes she plays too much.

While Karma is posting our pictures on 'MediaPal' I check my feed and I see yet again, the "pick me" female on Thomas' feed and him on hers. To me, she seems very desperate for his attention and it's working. He gives it to her, but in the beginning, when Thomas changed on me, and wouldn't talk as much as he did before, I was doing what the girl on his page is doing. The only difference is I did my desperation for his attention in the privacy of his inbox.

She is a pretty, young girl who seems nice from what I can tell from her posts, and she is a huge fan of his. I guess I am jealous because before we met, Thomas never said he loved me and give me pet names. When I think about my past conversations with Thomas, it started out with him opening up to me, checking on me, us messaging each other back and forth, and saying silly things to one another.

He was always on about his many projects and working out. He started from being chatty in my inbox to quiet and standoffish, and then it all stopped. So, when he did message me about coffee before I told him I was positive, I was shocked. Then I fucked it up again and told him about my HIV and he got silent... again. Well, young girl, Thomas and I fucked, so I think I just "one-up'd" you there. No, I'm kidding. Really. I am not that childish, and she seems like a sweet person. Us fans should stick together.

"Okay, let's take some together," says Karma.

"Let me get the phone tripod," I say as I run into my mom's bedroom, "Then we should leave after we're done."

We take a lot of crazy and sexy pictures the entire time she is here. Our phones blow up with all the likes and comments of the content we both upload. I didn't even get to put the Halloween decorations up like I wanted to.

"That didn't take long," Karma says with a playful giggle.

"No, but we need to go and beat the crowd. I'm sure many people aren't paying those parking fees either. I want to get there before the buses get crowded."

***

The first bus ride was nice and quiet, but once we get on the next bus that takes us straight to the pier, there are stares with "ohs and awes" and the smart asses.

"Halloween is just around the corner. You ladies couldn't wait, huh," says one male passenger.

"They look good though," says another.

Karma and I take our seats while laughing. The entire ride we talk and take more selfies. We also pose for pictures for a female passenger who loves our costumes.

We finally make it to the pier, getting off the bus feeling like superstars with all the attention we are getting. I haven't been to the pier in years. It looks like it had a makeover. We look for the entrance to see who made it.

"Wow, there are many people here already. Do you see Cash or Ming?"

"Oh, there is Terrell," Karma says as she heads his way.

It's crowded, and we are here ten minutes after the time the dance started. A handful of people are dancing while others are talking and checking out costumes. I turn a few heads while standing idle, since Karma left me for Terrell.

"Great costume, girl," says a woman who passes by with her group of family or friends.

"Thanks," I say with a smile.

The group is all in beauty queen attire with names on pageant sashes that represent their zodiac signs instead of states. I think it's pretty neat and unique how they did their sashes. Like they are competing on who is the best zodiac. I wish Karma could see this. She would love it!

"You all look good yourselves!"

"Why thank you," one woman says, "and vote Virgo!"

We all laugh before they go on their way.

As I am looking around at everyone, my eyes meet with Jason, who is walking through the entrance dressed as a vampire, and Kia next to him dressed as a playboy bunny.

Kia doesn't see me yet. She is busy looking around and being flirty with Jason, who has eyes on me. Oops, now she sees me. She makes her way to me with her hand firmly on Jason's arm.

"Uh... hi Kia."

"Hello, Vonne," she says with her usual grin, "I just want to say that your costume is hot!"

Now I know good and damn well she does not mean that. She walked her ass over here to say "I'm here with Jason" as if I will get upset, but I'll play this game with her.

"You both look good, too," I say, smiling.

"Alone, huh," Kia asks with sarcasm.

"I am here with the ladies, and they brought their dates."

I am still smiling, and I want her to see that she is not getting to me at all. Hopefully, it will work. She gets bored and leaves me alone.

"I meant a date," she says.

"I came alone. Maybe I'll meet a guy here tonight. I see a lot of fine ones standing around."

Kia looks like she is getting irritated with me now. She leans up for a kiss from Jason. It's a sad kiss and looks forced and awkward.

"Let's go, baby," she says to him as she wipes lipstick off of his mouth, "I want to look around."

"See ya," I say, still smiling.

Kia looks me up and down with disgust before she and Jason walk away. Jason is still looking back at me before finally focusing on Kia and whatever the hell she is saying to him.

I go out to the snack area where there is a line of vendors with food, drinks, and snacks, order a pizza puff with a Pepsi, and sit on a bench near the water. I eat alone and watch everyone have fun through the opening of the huge ballroom size area. Ming is with Jesse, laughing and holding each other. She is so beautiful in her costume, and Jesse seems pleased. Karma and Terrell are sitting at a small table away from the dance floor, having a submarine sandwich together.

I feel myself fill up with sadness. Here I am dateless and everyone else is looking good and having a ball. Then in walks Thomas, looking good as usual, wearing a Baron Samedi costume. I know it's him even with the painted skull on his face because of his walk and brownish wood-like bracelet he's always wearing. The costume fits him perfectly, but he looks good in anything he wears. Another giveaway is Renee, who is on his arm looking like she's dressed as Jessica Rabbit, and she is beautiful. I think she is the only black woman that can pull off full red hair. The red glittery dress, red lip, and stilettos also look good on her. She has exquisite, unblemished skin that is a light complexion. Or could it be full coverage makeup? Can never tell these days. They look very close and I doubt she is just a friend of Thomas who just wants company to an event. My stomach churns with a feeling of rocks and jelly to see them both together.

Thomas walks to the other end near where I am with Renee, and they sit down close to where Karma and Terrell are. They don't notice each other yet, but he notices me sitting alone.

He starts his way over after whispering something to Renee, but she pulls him back. He says something else to her and Renee nods and he walks over to where I am.

"Hi, Vonne," Thomas says, "You look beautiful."

"Thank you," I respond. "You look fantastic yourself!"

Thomas reaches out for my hand, helping me up from the bench. He then embraces me firmly while one hand is slowly caressing me down my back. My thoughts are racing. "Huh? I'm confused. He can't do this! Not now!" When I feel his smooth full lips on my neck, I completely give in. My soft moans make his kisses more powerful, and my body's response is to release a waterfall that I can't control. Why does he keep doing this? Where is Renee? I try to pull away, getting his attention. He stops but doesn't release me. His arms are around me and all I can think about is what happened that night we were together and why we can't officially be together now.

"Why are you out here alone," Thomas asks, pulling me back into his arms. "I saw your friends inside."

"I just came to eat and look at the water, but, Thomas, what the hell was that?"

"I don't know why I'm like that when I'm around you, Vonnie."

I'm sad and confused. I try to act like I'm cheerful, but my heart is aching because Thomas is with Renee and not me. Here we were just making out, but we are supposed to be just friends. Me and Thomas are going to have a serious chat after this dance!

Renee suddenly appears behind Thomas. The look on her face tells me she does not like the connection between Thomas and I. Or did she just witness what Thomas and I were doing? She has nothing to worry about. Now that I think I know that Thomas and Renee are together, because I'm not buying that story that it's just company, I will respect what they seem to have. Even when he comes at me with these little... I don't know what to call them. But I'm putting my foot down when I can have a moment with him to talk about this.

"Is everything okay," Renee asks while glaring at me.

"Yeah, yeah. Everything is cool." Thomas answers as he steps out of our embrace.

"I want to go see what they have to eat," Renee says.

She gives me a look of "back off". I look back at her but say nothing.

"Alright, well, I'm glad to see you, Vonne. Go try to have some fun."

I nod, and both Renee and Thomas head for the line of food carts.

I turn back to the water, then change my mind and instead go say hi to the girls. I see Cashmere emerge from the crowd with Troy and they are heading to where Terrell and Karma are, so I walk over.

"Hey, girl," Karma says, "we were looking for you."

"I was with Jason and Kia. Kia came over to fuck with me and I didn't react to her nonsense, so she left me alone."

Both Karma and Cashmere roll their eyes.

"Jason couldn't keep his eyes off me," I continue, "and I don't think Kia liked that, so she tried to show her ass and failed miserably."

"I can't stand that bitch," says Cashmere. "Why does she even care if Jason is still eyeing you. She probably has a line of men she is messing with right along with him."

"Well, that is his problem now," I say with a shrug.

"Hey, Miss Fairy," says Cashmere, "Hey, Jesse.!"

"Sup," Jesse says. "Good seeing you all again."

"I was looking for you," Ming says.

We hug, and I tease her about the huge, sparkly wings I see she decided to wear.

"Ooh, my song," Karma says with rhythm in her shoulders. "Come on Terrell let's go dance."

Donna Summer "Hot Stuff" is playing. Karma and Terrell are first on the dance floor, and Cashmere follows with Troy. I stay at the bench where Karma and Terrell sat, swaying to the music.

"Come dance, Vonne," Ming demands, pulling me with her to the dance floor, with Jesse not far behind.

Everyone else is strutting and sauntering onto the floor. I can't help but to dance. The music is loud, and it's making my body move to the thumping bass. I see Thomas and Renee dancing and enjoying themselves. Kia is dancing while Jason is watching but isn't dancing himself. I see a guy nearby with eyes on me, but seconds later, a woman appears by his side, and they dance together. No matter, I am enjoying myself. Ming and I dance together, laughing and twirling each other around. Maybe it's not so bad here.

The DJ continues playing hit after hit. All this dancing and I will lose this extra weight I'm sure I gained after the weekend I had everyone over. Those were no diet meals.

My mood quickly changes now that K-Ci and JoJo's "If You Think You're Lonely Now" play.

The song leaves me standing on the dance floor while all the couples slow down and dance close. Looking at Kia and Jason, I can't help but wonder if I would have forgiven Jason, would we be here together? Kia isn't nor will she ever be relationship material, but she is here with someone, and I am not, and that someone was my miracle. We are both going through the same thing, and I didn't have to worry about transferring the virus to him or him not being with me because of it. Now, all of that is over because of how he showed his ass instead of sitting down and talking to me about it. I look at Jason and, in my head, I am screaming "why".

Ming isn't far away. She looks so happy. She and Jesse are a blessing, and they are going strong. I'm so glad for her. I see the sparkle in her eyes as she holds on to Jesse. A sparkle brighter than any glitter or crystal on the costume she is wearing. She needs this and deserves it and I hope it lasts.

I ease away slowly, without Ming or any of my friends noticing. I sit in a chair by the exit leading out to the food stands. Hopefully, they will play something that I don't need a dance partner for.

Thomas and Renee aren't far from where I am sitting. The look that he gives Renee while his arms are around her tiny, cinched waist makes me heartbroken and I feel pangs of lighting striking my heart repeatedly. My stomach is in knots. What was all that earlier? If he is into me the way that he says, why is he smiling and looking into Renee's eyes? I finally was able to meet my crush, at least, huh?

He looks at Renee as if she is a princess character out of one of those fairytale movies. Renee's smile is wide and bright, looking back at Thomas like she is under a spell by his eyes. That's when I feel a lone tear fall down my cheek.

I can't be here. This is too much and at any moment, I will be sobbing, and I don't want to ruin the night for everyone because of my sadness. I see a bus that will take me to my second transfer, still sitting at the nearby turnaround station. I rise from my seat as I am wiping my tears away and quietly head for the exit, where just outside waits a line of buses.

***

When I board the bus, I take off the headband and wig and look for my card to pay.

"Are you okay, Ma'am," the female bus driver asks.

"No, but I will be soon enough."

I find my card and pay the fare. The bus is empty, and I choose a seat near a window where the huge open exit is. I can only see Ming, Jesse, Renee, and Thomas. All are still dancing and not notice I have left. That is what I want. Have fun, guys.

Once I walk in my door, the tears rush out like an overflowing dam has burst. I am so unhappy, and all the emotions hit me like a ton of bricks. I don't like the situation I'm in and instead of me moving on with someone else; I am still stuck on Thomas.

I close the front door and slide down into a fetal position on the floor nearby and let all my thoughts and memories of Thomas flow through warm tears that I can no longer control.

I finally rise, tossing the headband and wig that I still have clutched in my hands, and let my hair down out of the tight bun. I sit at the kitchen table, and I replay tonight's dance over and over. Mostly the part where Thomas and Renee are together. I get this overwhelming urge that I just want everything to be over. Not sure what happens when you die, but I want a do-over! I reach into a nearby drawer and pull out a pen with some paper. My tears are still flushing heavily, that I am blinded. I wipe them as I write a letter to my mom.

"Mama, I love you so much, and I'm so happy that I could meet you. You have done it all on your own, giving me the best care and love possible. I'm so sorry that I am about to destroy the precious gift that you have given me, and that gift is the decision to have me and bring me into this world. I tried, Mama. I tried so hard to live life and to be happy, but I can't. I tried every way possible to cure my depression, my sadness, and my fear of life, but I just can't. I am so sorry.

Please don't be mad at me. I will love you always. I just cannot do it anymore."

Some of my tears saturate the corner of the paper, but I don't care. I prepare the envelope and stick it in my mailbox for the mail carrier to pick up next week.

I return to the kitchen and start again. Only this time, I'm unsure if I can go through with it, at least until the images of tonight pop back into my mind, reminding me of why I'm doing this.

"Thomas, I am so glad to have met you. You are a wonderful man and although we didn't end up together, I wish you well on any lucky woman that you choose to be with. Please don't think I did this because of your decision, because it is deeper than that. Your decision may have helped me go over the edge, but not on you alone. I don't want you to feel guilt. I want you to do what you do and live your best life. You already know how I feel about you, and that will never change, which is why it's so hard for me to be around you and to see you with another woman. It's not your fault. It's mine and the choices that led me to this miserable place in my life, and I just can't be here. It is torture, and it hurts my heart so much because this virus is keeping me from love and that love is with the man I fell for. I am so sorry, Thomas. Please forgive me."

As I'm about to start my last letter, I put down the pen and lay my head on the cool kitchen wooden table. Ming and I have been through a lot, and not only do I feel like I'm abandoning my mother, but I feel I am also abandoning my best friend, too. She is the only one of my friends who knows me and what I am going through. We are both going through it. Is it selfish what I'm about to do? Or is it selfish that people force me to live a life for them even though I'm not happy with it? Raising my head, I check my phone before continuing. No messages from anyone, which only means they are still having a good time. With that, I write my last letter.

"Ming, I write this letter to you because you have been there, and you know everything about me. I am sorry I didn't say goodnight before leaving. I didn't because everyone was having a good time and I left because I couldn't stand the sight of Thomas and Renee. They look so happy and it's fine. I tried to live with me and Thomas only as friends but, Ming, I can't do it. I just can't. I wanted so much to be the woman in Renee's place, Him holding me, looking into my eyes. I just couldn't stay."

"Thomas loves me, Ming, but he is ignoring it as best he can because I'm positive. This is torture for me. Tonight, at the dance, he showed his affections to me yet again. So how can he smile and laugh with another woman if he loves me? It doesn't matter. I'm about to end the confusion, anyway."

"I will miss you Ming, and I love you very much. Thank you for being there for me and I'm so sorry that I am giving up like this. Please tell Cash and Karma I will always love them. I can't do this anymore."

I am sobbing more at this point. I just want this done. I grab a bottle of vodka that has been sitting in the bottom cabinet for as long as I can remember and found my mom's pain killers she uses for her injury and grab them, along with the letters I wrote to Ming and Thomas. My stomach is doing flip-flops as I and head for the living room. Not because I'm scared to die, because I'm not, but because I'm wondering if I'm doing the right thing.

I sit everything on the coffee table. It's odd that I'm not scared. I feel that leaving life will finally bring me peace and end this ongoing torment. I don't know where I will go once; I leave here. I just want out.

My phone is ringing, but I don't answer it. I imagine it's my friends finally realizing that I have left.

Ignoring the phone, I open my mom's bottle of pain medication and swallow the entire bottle of what's left of the pills inside and follow it with a few swallows of vodka. I replay my life as I continue taking huge chugs of alcohol. My thoughts are interrupted by the phone ringing again. It stops nothing. I just continue to drink.

It feels as if thirty minutes have passed, and my vision gets very cloudy. Tears are still pouring down my cheeks as I continue drinking. Even when I feel queasy, and I can no longer sit straight. Moments later, I fall over to the side, and I feel the liquor bottle slide out of my hand. I manage to lift my legs onto the sofa, and I wait for a better place. A place better than where I am now. I welcome it. My eyes are getting heavy, but my vision is steady. I hear my bell ringing. "Not now," I'm thinking, "Just let me go before they come in."

I can hear Ming. Her voice sounds as if she is far away. I hear footsteps rush in. I must've forgotten to lock the door when I set Mama's letter in the box. Damn it!

I see my friends and their dates, all looking as if they are running to me through clouds. Thomas is peering over Ming, sees my state, and rushes to my side while Renee is back behind the commotion with a look of annoyance. I hear my best friends, Ming and Karma, call my name over and over in tears. Cashmere falls to the floor in shock and Troy tries to help her up while looking on in disbelief. I can't make out where the other men are.

Thomas grabs my hand, sobbing while screaming at me. "Vonne, what did you do?! What did you do?!"

"I'm sorry," I say weakly, "Please just let me go."

"Call 911 now," Ming screams. "Bestie, stay with me! Don't go! We will get through this together!"

I open my mouth to tell her I love her, but I can't. My body is becoming heavy as my vision turns to darkness.

About the Author

Gem has only been an author for a short time and loves all the possibilities her imagination can take her. When she writes, she likes for her stories to stand out, trying to stay away from the "norm".

She lives in the Midwest and enjoys watching anything paranormal. Writing can be hard on her because of some memory loss, but she continues to share her stories. It's part of her relaxation and has been doing it for years. Although she has many manuscripts done, "Trust and Truths" is her first and only book published.

Hey you! I hope you've enjoyed my book. As a first-time author, I am excited to read what you liked about this story. I also welcome all criticisms. I want my readers to know that I take their reviews, words of encouragement and insight very serious. It will help me along the way as I write more stories for you.

-Gem

Acknowledgments

To my sweetest mom, my biggest supporter. We used to sit and talk about us both writing. You wanted to write children's books, and I would write whatever came to mind. You didn't get a chance at your dream of writing and I thought I wouldn't either, but you encouraged me to pursue mine, even if it was later in my life. Besides being my supporter in my writing, you are also the greatest mom for being there in everything else. When dad died, you kept everyone and everything together even when you were hurting. You think that your children and grandchild don't listen, but we do. Sometimes, we just want to see for ourselves, and when it doesn't go our way, we say "Mom was right". You did your best in raising us and even now you still do that. I'm so glad that this book published and because you were there and helped me when I needed most with this project, this is *our* book, Mom. So, we did it! I love and thank you.

To Dr. Jenny Lee, who helped me by suggesting I put my feelings on paper. Remember when we first met? I was broken physically and mentally. My injuries were terrible, and I was so down about it. Even after your help with everything, I still wasn't myself. You said it helps to write in a journal when I'm feeling depressed. Well, instead of writing about myself and feelings, I've decided to make my own characters that need help so that I can save them. It works out better than a journal because it gives me something to do and it's fun and relaxing, too! I'm really glad our paths have crossed, Dr. Lee. Thank you for everything.

My sister, Nicole, and son Larry, it means a lot that you both support my book even though you don't enjoy reading. Maybe I'll have an audiobook done just for the both of you. To be honest, Larry, you could give those video games a rest and read more. Or, you could've done an outstanding drawing for the cover. You have talent and it's a shame we didn't get a chance to work together. I love you both!

My aunts Vera and Yvonne. Vera, you helped in so many ways from helping me get everything ready so I could get started to starting a drawing for my cover. I'm sad that we weren't able to work together. I really wanted to have your art for the book. Yvonne, you cheered me on and kept me going. You were proud of everything that I did with my projects. Thank you both for your support and I love you.

Doris Jean, my sister from another mister. Like my mom, you were there with me through the stress of it all, even while you had a lot going on. Taking time out to proofread and edit for me. You are so busy with so much and you still find time to help when you can and support me. I love and thank you, sis!

A huge thanks to the anonymous people that helped with the research of HIV and how it affected you or someone close to you. Without you, I wouldn't have the information needed to create this story. I appreciate the time you spent with me and helping my characters with their backgrounds.